*A Royal Christmas*

featuring *Waiting for a Duke Like You* and

*A Prince in Her Stocking*

*Shana Galen*

*Waiting for a Duke Like You*

## Chapter One

Vivienne stumbled into the clearing and fell to her knees. The wet grass soaked through her skirts, but she barely noticed. Darkness still shrouded what she imagined in the sunlight were rolling green hills and manicured lawns.

Daylight was long, terror-filled hours away.

And she was so very, very tired.

She'd been running all night, running and hiding. She couldn't afford rest. The assassins were right behind her, hunting her. But for that hollow under the tree in the woods, they would have her now. She could not pause, not even for a moment.

She needed water. Her throat felt coated with sand, and it took effort to swallow. Since Masson had been murdered, she'd been constantly hungry and thirsty. She'd come this way because she thought she smelled water, and now looking out over the lawn that sloped down from the woods, she spotted a small pond with a charming bridge crossing it. The pond was not big enough to warrant a bridge, but it was probably an idea one of the British nobles had liked and commissioned. These nobles had more money than they knew what to do with.

Once she had been the same.

Looking left and right before moving further into the clearing, Vivienne made her way toward the pond. She had to restrain the urge to rush to the water and gulp great handfuls as soon as she reached the bank. Instead, she circled the pond until she faced the woods and her back was to the bridge. The shadows cast by the bridge in the weak light from the crescent moon would hide her, shield her, give her a moment to recover her strength.

With a last look at the woods, she removed her quiver and bow, set them against the bridge. She knelt and cupped the cool water, sniffing it and then drinking. She cupped more water, drinking and drinking until her empty belly roiled. Splashing water on her face, her arms, she rinsed some of the mud from her skin. Vivienne had hidden in a pigpen most of the day, and though the sow and her piglets had not seemed to mind her company, she was eager to leave reminders of the pigs behind.

She leaned against the bridge, bracing her weary body against the smooth, round stones. She'd been safe hidden under the pig muck. It wasn't until she'd tried to sneak away from the farm that the assassins had spotted her and come after her. Vivienne harbored no illusions that if the three men had caught her they'd leave her alive. They'd slit her throat just as they'd slit Masson's.

Poor Masson, she thought, closing her eyes against the sting of tears. He'd given everything he had to save her. She would not diminish his sacrifice by failing now. She had to reach London and the king. How far was Nottinghamshire from London? Hours? Days?

At the moment, London felt as far away as the moon.

She leaned her head back, eyes still closed. She would rise in a moment. She would keep moving south, south toward London. She would not rest until she reached the capital. She…

Vivienne slept.

***

Nathan Cauley, the Duke of Wyndover swirled the port in his glass. "I already have more money than I need. What I don't have is an heir. How I envy Hardcastle that nephew of his. Why can't I find a nephew and heir? Instead I've a cousin in the bloody Americas. My mother is on the verge of faking her collapse in order to hurry me along."

His host for the house party, the Duke of Sedgemere smiled. "There are worse things than matrimony, Nat."

"Says the man already leg-shackled. Besides, Elias, your duchess is one in ten thousand. Where am I to find a lady like her?"

"Do you know what your problem is?"

Wyndover drained the last of his port. "I'm sure you will tell me."

"You've had it too easy. You're a duke, and not just a duke, a young duke. Add that pretty face to the package, and the ladies fall all over you. All you need do is crook your finger."

"I object."

"On what grounds?"

"I have never crooked a finger at a lady."

Elias inclined his head, conceding the point. "My argument still stands. You have never had to woo a woman, never had to work to make one take notice of you."

"And *you* have? You're a bloody duke too, you know."

"If you think Anne merely fell into my arms, you don't know her very well. She led me on a merry chase, and I'm a better man for it."

"I'm too busy for chasing. Love and all that rot is fine for the likes of you, Elias, but I have estates to manage, solicitors at my door, stewards with rapidly multiplying rabbits."

"Rabbits?"

Wyndover waved a hand. "I need an heir, not romance."

"Then you haven't found the right woman yet. When you do, you'll welcome both the romance and the chase. You wouldn't have it any other way."

Nathan shook his head, but Elias did not stay to hear his protest. He stood. "I see Greenover is retiring for the night. There was an incident with a maid earlier. I think I'll make sure he finds his room without incident. I shall see you bright and early for the scavenger hunt, Nat."

Nathan gave his old friend a pained expression. "Scavenger hunt? Will your bride be very offended if I pass?"

"Try it and I'll call you out," Sedgemere said in a tone Nathan thought only half-joking. "This is her hostessing debut. You will cheerfully attend every single event and activity be it archery, embroidery, ices in the garden, or a scavenger hunt."

"Embroidery?"

"Be there with needle and thread."

Nathan gave a mock salute and watched his old school chum follow the lecherous Greenover out of the Billiards Room. If he'd been an intelligent man, he too would have sought his bed. Instead, Nathan poured another glass of port and settled back to watch Viscount Ormandsley lose yet another game of billiards.

The next morning came too early, and despite his tacit agreement with Sedgemere to act the dutiful guest, he was late for the start of the scavenger hunt. By the time he made it to the breakfast room, the other guests had already departed, all but a Miss MacHugh. He relaxed when he saw her. She had not fainted upon meeting him the day before. The same could not be said of two other ladies in the party—a Miss Frobisher and a Miss Pendleton. Miss MacHugh had not seemed particularly impressed by him, but then he'd seen her gaze slide to the Duke of Hardcastle one too many times.

Best he left Miss MacHugh to find her own amusements this morning.

He exchanged pleasantries with her then made his way to the drawing room to ask after the rest of the party. The butler informed him they'd already embarked on the scavenger hunt and handed him a sheet of foolscap on which had been listed a number of items he was to acquire.

"They have not been gone long, Your Grace," the butler said. "I am certain you will have no trouble catching up to one party or another and joining their ranks."

But that was the trick, Nathan decided. If he accidentally encountered the Frobisher-Pendleton party, he'd be stuck catching fainting ladies all morning and afternoon. He scanned the items listed on the paper.

*a horseshoe*

*a feather*

*a pink rose*

*a smooth, round stone for skipping*

The list went on and on.

He could find these items on his own, find them and complete the scavenger hunt without assistance or fainting ladies. He'd start with the skipping stone. It was in the middle of the list, and he imagined the teams would either begin with the first or last item and work from there.

He remembered crossing a small stone bridge upon arriving the day before. Several ducks had been swimming in a pretty little lake. He'd start there in his search for the stone. While everyone else swarmed the stables or gardens, he'd have a nice walk by the water.

Nathan started in the direction of the pond, encountering the Duke of Linton and Sedgemere's great-aunt, Lady Lavinia, returning to the house.

"Wyndover, join us" Lady Lavinia said, after the initial pleasantries. "I remember quite fondly a scavenger hunt with your late father. This was before he met your mother, and I rather think we spent more time flirting than hunting."

"Yes, do join us, Wyndover," Linton said hopefully, his voice raised so the deaf older lady could hear him.

"I wouldn't want to intrude," Nathan shouted. "I have my own plan of action."

Linton scowled, and Nathan made his escape, Lady Lavinia's voice carrying over the lawns. "Who is the object of his attraction?"

Nathan chuckled, crossing the lush green lawn quickly. Sedgemere's estate was well tended. As a man of property himself, Nathan noticed the details—the manicured flowerbeds, the way the land sloped away from the house to aid in drainage, the gravel paths which were free of weeds. He would have liked to see some of the surrounding land and meet a handful of Sedgemere's tenants, but that would have to wait until he'd played dutiful guest a few more days.

Sedgemere had mentioned archery, Nathan remembered as he neared the lake. God in Heaven, anything but archery.

At the edge of the water, he scanned the stones on the sandy bank. Several were quite smooth, but they were too round to skip well. He needed a stone flat and oval. He followed the edge of the water, head down, eyes narrowed for any sign of the perfect skipping stone. A duck quacked, and he looked out at the water, glinting in the morning sun. A drake, his mate, and a line of ducklings swam in the middle of the water, looking quite aimless. Doubtless the ducks were hunting insects for breakfast. He watched them for a moment but when he might have gone back to his search for skipping stones, his attention caught and held on a flutter of something brown near the base of the gray stone bridge.

It looked like a clump of brown cloth. A coat a groundskeeper had set aside and forgotten? He almost returned to his quest for the skipping stone, but something made him stare just a little longer. The coat was not empty. Someone was inside it.

Wyndover stuffed the sheet of foolscap in his coat pocket and walked rapidly toward the bridge. His long-legged gait ate up the distance quickly, and the indistinct shape became clearer. It was a body lying on its side under the shade of the bridge. As he neared the form, he made out the mud caked on the coat and the matted hair falling over the person's face. Probably a vagrant who'd fallen asleep there the night before.

At least Wyndover hoped the man was only sleeping. The last thing the Duchess of Sedgemere needed was a dead body to put a damper on her house party.

"Excuse me," he said as he walked the last few steps. "Are you hurt?"

The body didn't move. The wind ruffled the brown material again, but now Wyndover all but stumbled. It hadn't been a coat whipping in the breeze. Those were skirts.

A girl?

Where he might have nudged the body with his foot if he'd thought it a man, now he hunched down and examined the form. She did wear a coat—a man's coat—which was far too large for her small form. Beneath the hem of the coat, skirts covered with dry mud lay heavy against her legs, which were pulled protectively toward her belly. Her long dark hair covered her face, the muddy strands making it impossible for him to see her features.

Still, this was no lady nor one of the house party. She stank of shit and farm animals. Wyndover looked back toward the house. Should he fetch one of Sedgemere's servants? He winced at the thought. He could already hear the taunts from the other guests—*Leave it to Wyndover to find a girl on a scavenger hunt.*

*That was* gillyflower *on the list, Wyndover, not* girl.

*That desperate for a bride, Wyndover?*

He might not need to involve the servants, but he couldn't leave her here. "Miss." He shook her shoulder gently. It was surprisingly pliable under the stiff outer clothing. He'd expected to feel little more than bird-like bones. So perhaps she was not as malnourished as he'd thought.

"Miss," he said a little louder. He shook her again.

She moaned softly and then came instantly awake. He stood just in time to avoid her swing as she struck out. She scrambled up and back against the bridge, her arms raised protectively as though she expected him to attack. The matted hair fell to the side of her mud-streaked face, but her large green eyes stared at him with undisguised terror.

Wyndover raised his own hands in a gesture of peace. "I won't hurt you."

Her eyes narrowed. Such large eyes and so very green. They were the color of myrtle, a plant he knew well as he'd had to approve a hundred pounds for the purchase of myrtle at Wyndover Park. He'd stopped at his nearby estate before continuing to Sedgemere House and the head gardener had insisted on showing him the myrtle, which was in bloom with white flowers.

"Do you understand?" he asked when she didn't answer and she continued to look at him in confusion. "Do you speak English?"

"Yes." She rose, using the bridge to support her. "I understand."

Her voice held a faint exotic quality, a lilt that was both familiar and foreign.

She was no child; he could see that now. Although the coat hid her figure, he could see by the way she held herself she was a woman and one of some standing. She held her chin high in a haughty manner, and her gaze swept down him with an imperiousness he recognized from more than one *ton* ballroom.

She obviously decided he was no threat because her gaze quickly moved past him to scan the area around her. She reminded him of a hunted animal, a fox cornered by hounds. He wanted to reach out, lay a hand on her and reassure her, but he didn't dare touch her. The look in her eyes was too feral, too full of fear.

"Where am I?" she demanded, her eyes darting all around her, searching, searching. What was she looking for? What was she scared of?

"Sedgemere House," he answered. 'The residence of the Duke of Sedgemere."

"Are you he?"

If she didn't know Sedgemere she wasn't local. But if she didn't live in the area, then how had she come to be on Sedgemere's estate? He saw no evidence of a horse or conveyance. She must have walked. Another glance at the state of her clothing confirmed she must have been traveling for some time. Or perhaps not traveling but running. But from what or whom?

"No. Miss, you look as though you need some assistance. May I escort you back to the house?" Damn the taunts and teasing. The woman needed help.

She shook her head so violently flecks of mud scattered in the breeze. "I must be going."

She turned in a full circle, obviously trying to decide which way to travel. Her muddy hair trailed down her back, almost reaching the hem of the coat. Sections of it were still braided, indicating at one time it had been styled in some fashion or other.

"Which way to London?" she asked.

He almost answered. Her tone was such that he felt compelled to snap to attention as though he were the butler and she the master. Something else was familiar about her. The way she spoke, that accent. She wasn't English. Not French or Italian. He'd traveled the Continent years ago, when he'd been about two and twenty. He knew that accent, just couldn't place it at the moment.

"Why don't we discuss it inside over a cup of tea?" he said. "If you'll follow me—"

"I don't have time for tea. I have to run. Hide. They're looking for me. If they find me..." She shuddered and that one gesture said more than any word she'd spoken.

"Let me help you."

Her gaze landed on him again, ran quickly over him, and dismissed him just as quickly.

"If you want to help, tell me which way to London." She shook her head. "*Ne rien*! I'll find it on my own."

She swept past him, obviously intending to go on without his assistance. She might have climbed the embankment beside the bridge, but Wyndover suspected the exertion would have been too much for her. She would probably take the easier path around the pond and then double back and head south.

*Ne rien*. He'd heard that before, and quite suddenly he knew exactly where she was from. *Ne rien* was a Glennish phrase meaning *never mind* or *forget it*. Glennish was the mix of Gaelic and French spoken in the Kingdom of Glynaven.

He'd read reports of recent unrest in Glynaven. Another revolution ousting the royal family.

"Oh, bloody hell," he muttered as another thought occurred to him. He turned just in time to see her stumble. In two strides he was beside her, his arms out to catch her even as she fell.

He lifted her unconscious body, cradling her in his arms. She'd barely made it three feet before she'd collapsed from exhaustion. She might smell of manure and rotting vegetables, but with her head thrown back, he could see her face more clearly now. The high forehead and sculpted cheekbones, the full lips. She had all the features of the royal family of Glynaven.

But the unusual color of her green eyes gave her away—Her Royal Highness, Princess Vivienne Aubine Calanthe de Glynaven.

"Welcome to England," he said as he started back toward the house. She was light as a spring lamb, but he knew under the bulky clothing she had the full, supple body of a woman.

A beautiful woman.

She hadn't even recognized him. Other women might swoon at the sight of him, but her gaze had passed right over him, just as it had when they'd first met.

"You're in danger," he remarked to himself as he left the pond behind and started across the lawn. Not toward the house. He didn't dare take her to the house. One of the outbuildings. His gaze landed on a small shed, most probably a boathouse. He'd tuck her there and then fetch Sedgemere or his duchess.

"Princess Vivienne." He gave a rueful laugh. "Bet you never thought I'd be the one to save you."

## Chapter Two

She opened her eyes and blinked at the darkness. No, not darkness, she decided, but somewhere cool and dim. She hurt, everywhere. Her head felt as though encased in a helmet, and her legs and arms were leaden weights. She needed to sleep. She could sleep here in this cool darkness.

She closed her eyes again and everything rushed back at her—the revolution, the assassins, Masson's blood pumping out of his body...

She had to run, to hide.

She jerked up, thankful she'd been lying on the floor because her head spun. She rolled to her side, bracing her palms on the cool dirt and hung her head. Slowly, she gained her knees and began to push to her feet.

"Where do you think you're going?" a voice asked.

Vivienne jumped, her arms buckling and almost collapsing beneath her.

"You can't even stand. How far do you think you'll be able to travel?"

She turned her head, searching for the voice's source. He stood in a corner beside a row of oars that had been hung neatly on a wall. This wasn't a prison then. She glanced quickly about her, noting the watercraft. This must be where the nobles stored their boats, little more than rowboats, which made sense as the pond was too small for anything more substantial.

She put the pieces together, her head throbbing with the effort. She'd fainted—how absolutely mortifying! She had never fainted in her life. But she was so weak now and losing strength. As humiliating as it was to realize it, she knew she'd fainted, and he must have carried her here.

Why? To keep her until the assassins could be contacted?

She studied him again. No, she didn't think so. He was an Englishman. That didn't mean he couldn't be in league with the assassins. They must have some Englishmen on their side or at least willing to aid them for a handful of coins.

But this man was no farmer, no innkeeper. His clothes were too well made—a blue coat of superfine, a pale green waistcoat, a white linen shirt with an expertly tied neck cloth. He wore fawn-colored breeches and polished riding boots. The breeches were tight enough to mold to muscled legs.

She'd noticed that before—his broad shoulders, slim body, firm buttocks. But all of that was nothing when one took into account his face. He had the face of an angel. His skin was bronze; his cheeks smooth, and she imagined, soft and free of any stubble. His sunny blond hair fell over his forehead in a dashing sweep. His blue eyes were the color of the Mediterranean Sea before a storm and were framed by lashes several shades darker than his hair and thick enough that they provided a picturesque frame for eyes already striking.

No man should be so beautiful. If he'd been a woman, men would have fought wars for his hand. She hunkered on elbows and knees before him and felt like the lowest worm. She would have felt lacking beside him even had she been wearing her tiara and finest gown. She didn't like pretty men, didn't like men too vain to dirty their hands.

"Do lay back down before you fall," he said.

She shook her head. "I must go. I've lost too much time already."

"You'll lose even more if you collapse on the road."

This was true. Perhaps he did want to help her, and she would be wise to accept food and water. She hadn't eaten since yesterday morning and then only a crust of bread and weak wine.

"If you would be so kind as to gift me bread and cheese, I would be grateful. I have no money, but perhaps when I reach London, I could send you—"

He waved a hand, looking quite offended. "I don't want your money. I'm trying to keep you alive, Princess."

She started and fell back onto her behind. She would have been embarrassed if she hadn't been so shocked at his use of her title.

"How do you—?"

"You don't remember me?" He stepped away from the wall, into a thin shaft of light making a weak attempt to penetrate the spaces between the wooden boards that comprised the building's walls.

She didn't need the light to know his features. Should she know him? He did look familiar, now that she considered the possibility they'd met before. Not recently. Years ago, perhaps. But then she met so many people, so many men.

There were no counts in England. "Are you an earl?"

"A duke." He made a sweeping bow that would have perfectly graced her father's throne room. "The tenth Duke of Wyndover."

The name seemed familiar. If her head hadn't felt as though it would crack open at any moment and her eyes hadn't felt as though the lids were coated in sand, she might have remembered him. As it was, all she knew was that dukes had money and power. She needed food, a carriage, a coachman to take her to London.

Slowly, she rose to her feet, intent upon acting the princess even if it killed her. She wobbled, and he jerked as though he might help her. Something held him in check. Perhaps he knew her well enough to realize she wouldn't welcome him assistance.

"I thank you for your assistance, Duke. And since we are such old friends, I wonder if I might beg a favor."

"Old friends? You still don't remember me."

He sounded almost offended. Why should she remember him? He'd not been her lover nor had they ever kissed. They might have danced, but then she'd danced with thousands of men in the palace of Glynaven. She closed her eyes and willed the memories away. Memories of happier times.

"Of course, I remember you," she lied. "I couldn't place you at first. I'm not at my best at that moment." That was true enough.

He shook his head, clearly doubting her. "I suppose this is no more than I deserve."

He did step forward then and took her elbow. Out of habit, she began to jerk away. Before she did so, she realized she'd been tilting to the side and his grip had steadied her, prevented her from falling over.

"Do sit down, Your Highness. I've asked the butler to send the Duke and Duchess of Sedgemere, when they return. This is the duke's land, and he is a friend of mine. I instructed the butler to be discreet. You've stumbled upon a house party."

"I don't have time to wait for your friend. I must go before they find me. They will have no compunction about killing you, killing all of these people if it means they slit my throat in the end."

To her ears, her rapidly rising voice sounded hysterical, but he did not look at her as though she were mad. Instead, he gently lowered her to the floor, where she now saw he'd laid a burlap cloth of the sort one might use to keep dust off a boat.

"Who is after you? Does this have something to do with the political unrest in your country?"

*Political unrest.* Yes, that was one way to describe the revolution. That was a polite way to refer to the slaughter of her family before her eyes—her mother, her father, her siblings. They'd killed the royal family and all who were loyal to them. Vivienne had stumbled over the dead bodies of maids who'd done nothing more than launder her sheets. They hadn't deserved such gruesome deaths.

But the assassins were intent upon finishing what they'd begun in the revolution of ninety-eight. This time they intended to make certain no member of the royal family lived to hold any claim to the throne.

"Assassins," she said, her voice little more than a whisper. "They're searching for me. The head of the guard smuggled me out of Glynaven and brought me to Scotland. We'd made it as far as Nottinghamshire before the assassins caught up to us."

"And your guard?" the duke asked, though she could see in his eyes he'd already guessed.

"Dead." She looked down, blinked away the tears. "They're all dead."

She couldn't cry. Not now. Not until she had reached London.

His hand covered hers, and the warmth of his skin shocked her. She hadn't realized she was so cold or so desperate for any little morsel of human kindness. His warm fingers wrapped around her hand, and her heart melted at his touch.

She couldn't allow it though. If she softened now, she might never have the strength to reach London. She needed all her strength.

She tugged her hand away. "My hands are dirty."

He rose. Had she offended him? Quite suddenly she did not want him to go, did not want him to leave her. Her mother had always said she was a contrary child.

"I brought you a scone," he said, bending to retrieve a plate she hadn't noticed before. "I would have brought you more, something not as rich and water or tea, but I didn't want the servants asking questions—not until I'd spoken to Sedgemere, at any rate."

Her mouth watered when he removed the linen cloth from the top of the plate and she spied the lightly browned scone, smelled the scent of cinnamon and vanilla.

"Slowly," he said, raising the plate out of her reach. She hadn't even realized she'd reached for it. "You'll be ill if you eat it too fast."

She gave a quick nod, wanting the food more than she could ever remember wanting anything else in her life. He lowered the plate and she snatched the scone from it, turning away from him so he would not see her eat. Since she had no intention of losing the meager contents of her stomach, and she broke off a small piece and shoved it in her mouth.

She closed her eyes and chewed as slowly as she could, her hands trembling from the effort not to cram the rest of the scone in her mouth.

It was the best thing she had ever tasted in her life.

She ate another small bite then turned to the duke. "Thank you," she said, mouth full. It was the height of bad manners, but she didn't care. She could even feel the tears streaking down her face, tears of gratitude she couldn't hold back any longer.

He gave her a look of such pity, she would have hated herself if she had the energy. Instead, she broke off another small piece of scone and didn't protest when he pulled her into his arms. She should have protested. She should have chastised him.

*How dare you touch me without permission!*

But he smelled so absolutely wonderful, almost as lovely as the scone. He smelled clean, like soap and boot black and shaving soap. Comforting, normal smells. Scents she associated with her life before the revolution.

She should have stepped back. She was dirtying his clothing—very fine clothing from the feel of the wool against her cheek—with her mud-caked garments. Her body relaxed against his chest and she sagged into him, allowing him to support her. Just for a moment. She would stand on her own again, but she could lean on this man, this duke who had known her before her life had fallen apart, for a few seconds. His arms came around her. She was petite, and his touch—light, not possessive—wrapped around her back and shoulders.

"You're safe now," he murmured. "You're safe here."

And she believed him. She felt safe. For the first time in weeks she felt safe. She could lower her guard, relax her muscles, close her eyes.

\*\*\*

He was holding her. He'd never thought he'd hold her. And when he'd imagined doing so, he'd never imagined she would smell so disgusting.

But he didn't let her go. He might never have the chance to embrace her again, and he'd hold on as long as she'd tolerate it. He'd hold on forever because it would take a strong army to persuade him to let her go now. It was obvious she needed help, and he intended to do everything he could for her. She didn't remember him, and even if she had, she wouldn't have looked at him twice. Not the way he looked at her.

But this wasn't about winning her affections. He was a gentleman. He was honor-bound to aid a lady in distress. The feel of her in his arms was almost a reward in itself.

"My bow!" She jerked back, almost tripping over her own feet. He caught her arm, held her steady. "I left it. I have to fetch it!"

Pushing past him, she started for the door of the boathouse. It opened before she could reach it. The Duchess of Sedgemere entered, her gaze flicking first to the princess and then to Nathan.

She was a pretty woman and not one prone to hysterics. Her expression remained placid, despite the surprise she must have felt at seeing a strange, filthy woman in her boathouse with one of her house guests.

"Duchess," Nathan said smoothly, moving to block the princess from escaping and simultaneously shield her with his body. "I apologize for taking you away from your guests and the activities."

"Gladstone said you asked him to send the duke or myself to you right away." Her gaze slid from him to the princess at his side. "Is there a problem?"

"Yes, but I should make introductions first. Her Royal Highness, Princess Vivienne of Glynaven this is the Duchess of Sedgemere. It was her bridge I found you sleeping under. Duchess, this is Princess Vivienne. She's in a bit of trouble at the moment."

The duchess raised her brows with some skepticism, but she managed a very formal curtsy. "I'm pleased to make your acquaintance, Your Highness."

"Please, call me Vivienne. I'm endangering you, everyone here, with my presence. It's better if you don't use my title."

"Very well, then you should call me Anne, and I must insist you come to the house with me. You need a bath, clean clothes, and a good meal."

Vivienne shook her head. "Thank you, but no. As I said, my presence here is a danger to all of you. I only want to collect my bow and be away." She eyed the scone in her hand and ate another small bite, clearly unwilling to leave it behind.

"You can't leave," Wyndover said, surprising himself. The duchess's eyes widened, while the princess's eyes narrowed. He cut her argument off. "You're in no shape to travel to London, especially if you are being pursued by assassins."

"Assassins?" the duchess paled, but to her credit, she stood her ground.

"I will gladly accept the loan of a horse or conveyance," the princess answered, haughty as ever.

"And have the assassins take it away at the first opportunity? I think not."

Her green eyes darkened with fury. "I don't know who you think you are—"

"I'm a man who knows England a great deal better than you. You're a lone woman traveling on foot, even traveling on horseback, you have no protection. If these assassins don't attack you, someone else will."

"I agree," the duchess said. "A woman alone is not safe from thieves or highwaymen, and the closer you come to London, the more danger you face. You cannot go alone."

"And I cannot stay here."

"I'll take you," Nathan said. The moment the words were out of his mouth, he wanted to shove them back in again. What the hell was he suggesting? He couldn't take her to London. He'd traveled from Town for this bloody house party. He couldn't get involved in the revolutions taking place abroad. He had estates to manage, tenants to see to, ledgers to balance.

But he'd be damned if he allowed her to walk away from him. She'd be dead before the sun rose again. And if he had other reasons for wanting to stay with her, he didn't intend to examine them to closely.

"Fine," the princess said, surprising him. He'd fully expected her to argue, to say she didn't want him. "You may accompany me."

Nathan clenched his hands at her imperious tone.

"But you take your life in your hands, Duke. You have serfs depending on you."

"We don't call them serfs—"

"An important man like you must have fiefdoms. Can you really afford to risk your life to escort me to London? I think it's better if I go alone."

"That's out of the question."

"Fine, then fetch your carriage. We leave now."

The duchess pressed her lips together, clearly hiding a smile. She had noted the princess's dictatorial tone as well.

"That's also out of the question," Nathan said. He could dictate too. "A journey like this takes a bit of planning and preparation. Not to mention, I have no intention of traveling anywhere with someone who smells like pig feces—be she a princess or not."

"Why you—"

The duchess cleared her throat. "Your Highness— Vivienne—perhaps you might come inside and take the opportunity to wash and change. You're shorter than I, but I could ask my maid to hem one of my gowns or take it in a bit."

"Thank you, Duchess, but no," Nathan said. "If the assassins are tracking her, and I think we must assume they are, I want her far away from here, from your party, and the guests. There are children present, and we must think of their safety."

"Then what do you propose?" Vivienne demanded, hands on her hips.

"You come with me to Wyndover Park. It's only a couple hours' ride from here. That's far enough to put distance between you and your pursuers but close enough that I can have you there quickly. At this point, your safety is paramount."

Her expression was unreadable. It might have been the streaks of dirt on her face, but Nathan rather suspected she wasn't quite certain what to make of him. Good. He'd keep her guessing.

"How can I help?" the duchess asked.

"I want to leave without being seen. I'll need you to make my excuses."

"Of course."

Vivienne nibbled the scone while he and the Duchess of Sedgemere devised a plan. She would tell Sedgemere the truth, but everyone else would be told Wyndover had an aching head and had gone to his room. During the next activity, which was a picnic in the garden, Wyndover and the princess would slip away in his coach and return to Wyndover Park. That evening at dinner, when the duke and the princess were safely at Wyndover Park, Sedgemere would inform the guests Wyndover was called to his estate in Gloucestershire on urgent business. Nathan had thought it best to stick closely to the truth, and he instructed the duchess to say that a fire had broken out at one of the tenant's cottages. This was true, although the steward at the estate had the matter well under control—except for the small matter of housing the tenant's rabbits—and Nathan was not needed.

"I should return to the house before I am missed," the duchess said. "I wish you a safe journey."

"Tell Elias I'll write to him with news, and accept my apologies, Duchess, for my early departure."

She waved her hand as though his absence was nothing, although he knew it would upset her numbers and cause her some difficulty. "It was a pleasure to meet you Vivienne. I do hope we can meet again under better circumstances." She curtsied again and then she was gone.

Nathan leaned against the door. "I think it best if we stay here and out of sight until my coachman sends word that the coach is ready."

"I agree, but I must have my bow and arrows first."

"You always did love archery."

"And a good thing as my skill with a bow saved me any number of times. I even wounded one of the assassins in the leg. I had hoped his injury would afford me some time, but the others seemed to come even more quickly."

"How many are there?"

"At least three, but there might be more." She motioned toward the door.

"I'll go," Nathan said. "You stay inside and hidden. Where did you leave them?"

"I slipped them off before drinking and leaned them against the stone bridge. I must have fallen asleep, and when you woke me, I didn't think to gather them."

"I'll return in a moment."

He opened the boathouse door a crack, peered out. The duchess had returned to the house by now and no one else was about at the moment. Quickly, Nathan stepped outside and closed the door behind him. The bright sunlight made him squint, but he shielded his eyes and made his way back to the pond and the bridge where he'd seen her this morning.

He stayed alert, scanning the tree line and the lawns for any sign of movement. The pond was far enough from the house that he heard nothing and saw nothing. Finally, he returned to the spot where she'd been sleeping and circled the area, looking under the bridge and in a nearby patch of fuzzy swamp willows. He imagined her crouching down beside the water to drink, tracked his gaze to where she would have set the bow and arrows.

She would have wanted them close at hand when she sat to rest for a moment. Nathan stood again where he'd found her sleeping. He could still see the indentation of her body in the sand and in the middle of that hollow, a footprint.

There was no bow, no arrows.

Nathan put his own foot beside the print. His boot was larger.

Whoever had been here had tracked the princess, taken her bow and arrows.

And the assassins would keep tracking until they had her too.

# Chapter Three

"You don't know it was the assassins who took the bow and arrows," the duke said. He was seated across from Vivienne in his well-appointed coach, both of them resting on royal blue velvet squabs and using hand holds of gold silk.

"Yes, I do. You are fortunate the bow and arrows are all they took." He still had his life.

"I prefer a fight to running and hiding. I would have taken them too."

He would have given the assassins a good fight, of that she was certain. Unlike Masson, the duke was prepared for an attack, and he looked like the kind of man who could hold his own. British men liked to think of boxing as a sport. In her country it was much the same. But the assassins weren't gentlemen or bound by a code of honor. They intended to kill her, and they would do so by any means necessary.

Still, she was quietly grateful to the duke. His presence had saved her life. If he hadn't woken her, if he hadn't looked strong and formidable, she would be dead by now.

"They must have taken the bow and arrows while we were in the boathouse," she said. "If they'd come while I'd been sleeping, they would have killed me."

"Why not attack us in the boathouse? Why not kill you when I went back to the house to fetch the scone and speak to the staff?"

"I don't know."

"I will write to Sedgemere when we arrive at Wyndover Park. No doubt the bow and arrows will turn up at the house party."

She didn't agree, and the thought made the food in her belly—the duke had procured bread, cheese, and wine—sit like handful of stones. She'd had that archery set since she'd been sixteen. It had been a gift from her father on her birthday, and the two of them had spent many happy hours together shooting at targets, laughing, and competing.

And now he was dead.

She closed her eyes.

To her shock, Wyndover's gloved hands clutched her bare ones. Once again, she was aware of how dirty and unkempt she looked. His gloves were perfectly white, while her hands were black with grime.

"I can see the loss of the bow and arrows has upset you, but you don't need them any longer. I'll protect you. I won't allow any harm to come to you."

If he had been Glennish, one of her countrymen, she would have accepted his words without comment. It would have been his duty to protect her. But this man owed her nothing. Why should he risk his life for her? Why should he comfort her or dirty his hands for her?

"That is very kind of you," she said carefully. "Do you mind if I ask why?"

He did mind, at least she surmised as much when he released her hand and sat back. "Because you are in danger. What sort of man would I be if I did not help someone in danger?"

"A typical man," she said.

He folded his arms over his broad chest. The late morning sun sliced through the carriage windows, which he had insisted need not be covered, making his hair look even lighter and his blue eyes look almost clear.

"I don't agree. Most men I know would do no different."

"Then you have not spent much time at court. The men I know do nothing if it doesn't benefit them. I have been to the court of your King George when he was still well. I saw little difference."

He pressed his lips together, and she watched with an interest she could not quite control as they gradually released and became full again. She wondered what it would be like to kiss those lips, to caress those perfect cheekbones, to stare into those bluer than blue eyes. What kind of lover would this man be?

An unselfish one, she decided. The thought did nothing to distract her from the wayward path of her thoughts.

"I haven't spent much time at court, but I have been in Parliament for several years. Political expediency is the way of most powerful men, but that doesn't mean that they are not good men at the core."

She let out a huff of breath and looked away. Let him hold on to his naivety. She couldn't forget the carnage *political expediency* had wrought on her country, her family.

"I'll replace the bow and arrows for you."

She jerked her head to stare at him in astonishment. "You needn't do that."

"I want to. I recall how much you enjoyed archery."

"You seem to remember me very well. Why is it I have such a vague recollection of you?"

"It wasn't for lack of trying on my part. I tried to catch your attention, but you were politely indifferent."

She smiled. "That is an apt description, I suppose."

"Very apt. I'm not particularly witty or fascinating. I suppose I didn't interest you."

Poor man. He thought he'd bored her.

"I'm afraid there is very little you could have said or done to capture my attention, Duke. Even if you had been as amusing as

Leland Vibosette"—she said, referring to one of Glynaven's most witty actors—"I would not have sought you out."

"You find me distasteful in some manner?"

"No, not at all. I find you too much to my taste."

His brows came together in confusion. It made him look a good deal younger and quite adorable. Perhaps she had drank too much of the good red wine he'd given her on an empty stomach.

She gestured toward his face. "I don't like men who are more attractive than me. I suppose it's vain and shallow, but I like to be the pretty one."

His brows rose again, and he stared at her for a long moment. His eyes seemed to look right through her to the point where she wanted to shift with discomfort.

"I don't know what you look like under the mud and grime, but if it's anything like what you looked like when I first met you, you are the most beautiful woman I have ever seen."

She gasped in surprise at his words. She'd been complimented before, of course, but never had any man's words sounded so sincere, so heartfelt. There was almost a tone of anguish in his voice.

"That's not true," she whispered. "I'm short and dark."

"You are petite and your skin looks sun-kissed. Your hair is the most lovely shade of dark brown I have ever seen. But you are more than physically attractive. When I met you before, I found you graceful, well-spoken, and kind. Your servants could not praise you highly enough."

Her heart pounded so hard in her chest she had to press her hand to it. "You flatter me."

"No. I speak the truth. In all honesty, I would never have wanted any harm to befall you or your family. But I would be lying if I did not say I think I am the most fortunate man alive to have found you this morning. And I don't think it's merely coincidence."

"You think it fate?"

"I think I have another chance to make you see me as something more than a...*pretty* face."

"Then you have an ulterior motive for helping me too."

His eyes narrowed and his jaw tightened. "What have I done to deserve such an insult?"

"Nothing. I did not mean to imply—"

"Yes, you did. You think I help you because I hope to take you to bed, because I want some sort of payment from you?"

She didn't answer. That was exactly what she thought. Shame crept through her, making her face hot.

"I won't deny that I would rejoice if you fell completely in love with me, if you *wanted* me in your bed. But I would have helped you even if you'd been an ugly old crone missing half your teeth."

She believed him too. The force of his conviction was entirely convincing.

He looked away from her, his eyes on the countryside visible through the carriage windows. Vivienne was not often sorry, but this was one of those rare occasions. She found she wanted him to look at her again, to speak to her with that warmth in his voice. Instead, they sat in silence for the next hour until they reached Wyndover Park.

***

"Your Highness," Nathan said, as the coach came to a stop. "We have arrived."

He'd watched her fight to keep her eyes open, watched her lose the battle and fall asleep, her cheek resting on the squab. She must have been exhausted because she did not move. She slept like the dead.

He wished he had a wet cloth to wipe some of the dirt from her face. He imagined she looked lovely when sleeping. Soon enough she would be able to bathe and sleep in a bed. Perhaps that would restore her. In the meantime, he could make plans to travel to London.

Thank God his mother had left to spend the rest of the summer in Bath with her friend Lady Tribble. He did not want to have to explain his arrival with a princess of Glynaven in tow. As it was, he would have to think what to tell the staff. He was not expected to return after the house party at Sedgemere's residence, and the staff had been reduced accordingly. That meant fewer people to trust to keep quiet.

"Your Highness," he said again, a little louder this time.

Her eyes opened, so vibrantly green, and she sat stiffly. For a moment, she looked about in confusion. Finally, she notched her chin up. "We've arrived."

"Yes. Welcome to Wyndover Park."

She peered out the window at the front of the house where the coach had stopped after making its way down the long drive. He was the tenth Duke of Wyndover, and the house was an old one. It had been refurbished every hundred years or so, but it retained some of its ancient charm—turrets and towers and crenellated parapets.

The door opened, and he stepped out first, holding his hand to assist her. She took his hand, her gaze on the house.

"It's very grand," she said, looking up. "Very imposing."

"It was meant to be." He tucked her arm in the crook of his elbow and led her toward the door. "It was built for an ancestor of mine who was a baron. Wyndover Park—it was not called that then—was the sole protection for farmers and tenants when there was an attack. At one time there was a drawbridge and moat. Now only what would have been the keep remains. It has been modernized, of course."

"Of course." She paused just before they reached the door where he could see his butler Chapple stood just inside, waiting to greet him.

"I want to apologize," she said, "for my thoughtlessness in the coach. I impugned your honor, and you had every right to be angry with me."

"All is forgiven." He waved a hand as though to waft away the smoke of discord. "I'm not one to stay angry for long, and I can hardly blame you. After what you've been through, questioning men's motives mean survival."

She gave him another bewildered look. Soon enough she would take him at his word.

Nathan gestured to his man just inside the door. "My butler, Chapple. Good that you hadn't returned to London yet, Chapple."

"I was still putting the staff through its paces, Your Grace. I received word you would be returning and have made certain all of your requests have been granted. This, I presume, is the young lady who will be occupying the yellow room."

Nathan had seen the butler's gaze drift over the muddy clothes, but his expression remained respectful.

"Yes, Lady Vivienne"—he gave her a look rife with meaning—"my butler Chapple."

"My lady." Chapple bowed.

"I hope I didn't put you to too much trouble," she said.

"None at all, my lady. May I have the housekeeper show you to your room?"

"I'd like that."

"Perhaps the footmen might bring hot water for a bath."

"Yes, thank you."

"Is there any luggage?" Chapple asked him.

"Sedgemere will have mine sent with Fletcher. The lady has none."

"We might ask one of the maids to peer into Her Grace's dressing room, but I'm afraid your mother is a good deal taller than Lady Vivienne."

A good deal wider too, Nathan thought.

"Perhaps one of the maids might have a dress she could borrow until Lady Vivienne's might be laundered and returned."

"I will see to it, Your Grace." Chapple raised his hand and what Nathan assumed must be every servant in the house came forward. The princess was led away, surrounded by the housekeeper and maids while Chapple issued orders at the manservants in rapid succession.

Nathan's head hurt from the morning's exertions. He backed away, seeking the solace of his library. "Chapple, bring me every copy of *The Times* you can find," he ordered. "No matter how old."

"Yes, Your Grace."

"Have Cook send tea with brandy and…" What was it sick people ate to restore their strength? "And broth of some sort to Lady Vivienne's room after her bath."

"Broth, Your Grace?"

"Just do it, Chapple. Don't stand there staring at me. I want those copies of *The Times*."

Nathan stalked away muttering. "A man can't even request broth without his servants gaping."

Once in his library, he sat in his favorite chair beside the fire and propped his feet on a nearby table. His mother would have been appalled, but his mother was in Bath. Good thing too or else he would have been answering all of her pointed questions about the princess rather than enjoying a few minutes' solitude and quiet.

A brisk knock sounded on the door and Nathan dropped his feet. So much for solitude.

"Come."

Chapple entered, arms laden with newspapers. "*The Times,* Your Grace."

Nathan rose and took them. From the weight of them, he judged his butler had unearthed at least a dozen copies if not more.

"Is the—Lady Vivienne settled?"

"I believe she is enjoying the broth you requested, Your Grace." Chapple smirked. Nathan had never seen his butler smirk before, but he didn't know how else to describe the expression on the man's face at the moment.

"That will be all, Chapple. I don't wish to be disturbed."

"Would you like Cook to send broth for you too, Your Grace?"

Nathan gave the man a narrow stare, but Chapple blinked innocently.

"No. My usual fare will be fine. I'll have it in my room as I don't expect Lady Vivienne will be well enough to come down to dinner."

"Yes, Your Grace."

"One more thing, Chapple."

Nathan hesitated to mention additional security measures. He'd always been perfectly safe and at home in his Nottinghamshire estate. However, if assassins really did roam the countryside, searching for the princess, it was better to act proactively.

"I am not expecting any guests. Admit no one while Lady Vivienne is here. If anyone comes to call, I am not at home. I would also ask you to instruct the servants not to mention Lady Vivienne's presence here for the moment. I rely on the staff's discretion, Chapple."

The butler stiffened. "Of course, Your Grace. As you should."

Nathan went back to his chair and wished he could lift the papers and begin sorting through them. But he had better finish this.

"Lastly, I want everyone on their guard. I've…heard rumors of some rather unsavory characters in the area. I want everyone to take precautions and to alert me if they see anyone unusual or unfamiliar."

"Absolutely, Your Grace." Chapple wrung his hands together, his concern obvious. Nathan would have preferred to avoid alarming the staff, but he could not be too careful.

"Is it highwaymen again, Your Grace?" he asked, referring to the highwayman who had preyed on the shire the Christmas before last.

"No. Nothing like that. Be watchful, Chapple. That's all I ask."

When he was alone again, Nathan perused the editions of *The Times*. The first few held no information of interest, but a quarter of the way through the stack, he found an article on the unrest in Glynaven.

British citizens traveling in the country reported unrest among the populace, stirred up by various anti-monarchist groups. There had been a revolution in the late 1700s, quite a bloody one from the accounts Nathan had read. After that uprising a military government had taken power, but the people soon revolted again and demanded the return of the monarchy. Vivienne's father was the brother of the deposed King, and he had taken the throne about fifteen years before.

Nathan found another article about the royal family. It didn't mention the princess but stated that King Guillaume was much loved. His rule had been characterized by peace until a growing faction of revolutionaries had begun to call for his abdication. Many of them had crossed to Glynaven from France, a country that had undergone its own violent revolution not long before.

Liverpool, the Prime Minister, and the Prince Regent had not made any comment on the worsening situation in Glynaven. Nathan suspected they did not want to cause friction or appear to take sides. Was Vivienne fooling herself by thinking she would be safe if she reached London? Would the King really give her sanctuary or would he wash his hands of her and leave her to fend for himself.

The King might have never acted so dishonorably, but it was the regent who held the reins of power at the moment. Prinny was selfish and self-serving. Nathan thought it unlikely he would come to Vivienne's rescue.

Finally, Nathan found an article on the revolution itself. The paper was only a few days' old and the actual assault on the palace in Glynaven had taken place only a fortnight before. Eyewitness accounts were still being collected, but most agreed that the rebels had stormed the castle and murdered the royal family in their beds. The bodies of the king, the queen, and two of the four princesses had been identified. Two other bodies of women were presumed to be Vivienne and her sister Camille, but the corpses were so mangled identification was difficult. The body of a man presumed to be the crown prince had also been found, but again, due to the state of the body, identification was a challenge.

Nathan set the papers aside and raked a hand through his hair. How had Vivienne managed to escape? And what horrors had she seen before she'd fled? It was a wonder she was still alive, a wonder he'd been entrusted to keep her safe.

He heard the clock chime on his desk and looked over. It was late, later than he'd anticipated. He was hungry and tired. Nathan wanted to speak to Vivienne, to discuss her plans to travel to London. It would have to wait until morning.

He made his way through the familiar rooms of Wyndover Park and up the winding marble staircase to his room. The yellow room, where Vivienne was housed, was at the end of the corridor. It was the most comfortable of the guest rooms and had the added benefit of being far enough away from the ducal bedchamber so as not to tempt him to knock on her door.

His dinner arrived a few minutes later. Nathan ate it but dismissed his valet after Fletcher helped him remove his coat. Alone, Nathan flung the material of his neck cloth on the floor and stood at the window in shirtsleeves, looking out at the encroaching darkness. The sun did not set until late in the summer months, and only now did shadows begin to obscure his view of the gardens.

He supposed he should sleep and had just pulled his shirttails from his trousers when he heard the screams.

## Chapter Four

When the alarm sounded, Vivienne had run to the hiding place. She'd been awake, even though it was long after midnight, because she'd wanted to finish a book.

Mr. Wordsworth had saved her. If she'd been sleeping she might not have heard the alarm or not been fast enough. She was the only one of her family to make it to the small, unassuming sitting room in one corner of the palace where a hidden room lay behind the portrait of her grandfather. She'd waited anxiously for her sisters, her parents, her brother to slide the painting away from the wall and creep into the stone space with her, but no one ever came.

When she heard the clang of steel and the cries of pain, she prayed her family would come. She prayed they'd escaped through other hidden passages, though those were few and difficult to reach. Instead, she sat shivering for what seemed days and days while the terror erupted around her. In truth it had probably been only hours.

It had taken but a few short hours to murder the occupants of the palace, to rape and pillage, to destroy what had once been lauded as the most beautiful royal residence on the Continent.

At some point the next day, Masson had pulled her, shaking and nauseated, from the hiding place. She didn't know how he'd managed to avoid the carnage or how he'd sneaked into the palace to rescue her. She only knew he looked haggard and ten years older than he had when she'd seen him less than twenty-four hours before.

"Your Highness, the *reavlutionnaire* have taken over the country. If you are to live, we must sail for Britain now. Today."

"My mother?" she'd croaked. "Papa?"

Masson shook his head sadly. He'd been her father's advisor for over a decade. She knew he felt the loss almost as keenly as she did.

Vivienne had sobbed and Masson had permitted it for a few moments, and then he'd taken her by the shoulders. "You must be strong now, Princess Vivienne. The *reavlutionnaire* are in the taverns, celebrating their victory. They will return, and when they realize you are not among the dead, they will look for you."

Vivienne nodded and took Masson's arm. She couldn't indulge her grief, not when she was the last of her family. Not when any delay could mean not only her death but the death of Masson. At the door to the ransacked sitting room, Masson paused.

"Do not look, if you can avoid it, Your Highness. The *reavlutionnaire* spared no one."

But of course she had seen—men, women, children. All dead. Blood everywhere. Gaping wounds. And eyes. So many sightless eyes.

She'd taken no more than a hundred steps before she saw her mother's body. The queen had been trying to escape to the safe room. She'd never made it. More sightless eyes.

And then, just days ago, Masson's glazed eyes staring at her when the *reavlutionnaire* had come for her in a barn in Nottinghamshire. She'd hidden in the hayloft, and when the *reavlutionnaire* had gone out to look for her, she'd had no choice but to pass his body. To feel the sightless eyes on her.

So many eyes staring at her, accusing her.

*Why aren't you one of us? Why did you live?*

The voices rang in her head, and she covered her ears to drown out the sound, screamed and screamed until she couldn't hear them any longer.

One of the bodies rose up and grabbed her shoulder, shaking her. It spoke to her, but Vivienne clawed at it, fought it.

"Vivienne!"

She fell, and when she opened her eyes she lay in bed, the sheets tangled around her, the room yellow from lamplight.

She stared at the unfamiliar face, stared at the impossibly handsome man kneeling over her. His face was so close to hers that she could practically see the dark blue rim of his iris. She felt the fine lawn between her fingers and followed her arms to where she clutched his shirt.

Abruptly, she released him, and he moved back and off the bed.

"*Je sui duilich.*"

"You have nothing to apologize for," he answered in English. His eyes were very blue and his face pale with concern. Her throat felt raw and parched, and she realized she must have been screaming for several minutes if he had been concerned enough to enter her room.

He motioned toward the door, and several women in caps moved back. The maids must have heard her as well. She'd probably awakened the entire household. She felt her face heat and wished she could bury herself under the covers.

Of course it was at that point she realized she was naked and the sheet only barely covered her breasts. She ruched it up to her chin and glanced at Wyndover. His focus was on the servants in the doorway.

"The lady is fine now, as you see. A nightmare. We can all return to our rooms."

With a murmur of feminine voices, the maids withdrew. Wyndover bowed to her and backed toward the door. "May I fetch you anything, Lady Vivienne?"

She shook her head, her throat too raw to speak.

"Good night then." At the door he paused, glanced behind him. "We need to talk," he hissed in a whisper. "I'll return in ten minutes."

And he was gone.

Vivienne fell back on her pillows. If she hadn't still been shaking from the dream, she would have been mortified that her screams had awakened an entire household. A duke's household, no less. As it was, she wanted to pull the covers over her head and hide from the memories.

But she was a princess, and she had to behave as such.

The maids had found a simple day dress for her to wear, but she didn't want to call them to help her dress. Instead, she wrapped the sheet around her body and dangled her legs over the side of the bed. For weeks all she'd thought about was fleeing to London. London was safety in her mind.

But was it really? Would she be safe anywhere with the dreams and memories haunting her?

London was no different than anywhere else. The assassins could find her there. She would not be safe while they wanted her dead. Even King George could not protect her forever.

If he protected her at all.

A quiet tap on the door made her jerk her head up. Wyndover peeked inside holding a lamp. Seeing her sitting on the side of the bed, he entered and shut the door soundlessly behind him.

"How are you feeling?" he murmured, keeping his voice low.

"Better." Surprisingly, she meant it. When she was in his presence, so many of her fears seemed to dissipate. "Better now that you're here," she said.

He didn't reply, but his gaze stayed focused on her, those bluer than blue eyes studying her face. Then his gaze slid down her neck, and she felt the heat of it on her bare shoulders and through the thin sheets over her breasts, her stomach, her hips, thighs, legs, until his gaze rested on the naked feet and ankles hanging exposed.

"We should speak tomorrow." His gaze returned to her face. "I jeopardize your reputation with my presence."

For a long moment she was not certain what he meant. But of course the English had different customs and traditions than the Glennish.

"In Glynaven, a lady's reputation is not so difficult to tarnish. Virginity is not so highly prized."

"I know."

Of course he did. He had been to Glynaven.

"You're not in Glynaven any longer." He looked at the door as though contemplating withdrawing.

"Stay with me for a few moments." Panic bubbled inside her at the idea of being alone again with only the sightless eyes for company.

"Won't you?" she added, when his jaw tightened.

She might be a princess, but this man was no underling she might order about. She patted the spot on the bed beside her and gave him what she hoped was an inviting smile.

He studied her again—definitely a man who took time with his decisions—and then placed the lamp on the bedside table and stood before her. He made no move to sit beside her. Perhaps that went too far for his British sense of honor.

"I spent the evening reading accounts of the revolution. I'm sorry about your family."

She inclined her head in a gesture she'd mastered by the age of two. "Thank you."

"Was it very bad?"

When she blinked at him, he cleared his throat. "I meant your nightmare. Was it very bad?"

"Bad enough." She couldn't speak of it. Her body wanted to shudder at the mere thought of those sightless eyes. She suppressed the instinct and swallowed hard. "I am better now."

Much better with him so close, his shirt open at the throat and rolled at the sleeves. That bare expanse of his bronze neck made him somehow more vulnerable. She had the urge to touch the skin there, to kiss it and the golden stubble on the base of his jaw. Instead, she wound her hands together, pressing the fingers tightly.

"You're safe here," he said. "I've ordered a man to be on guard at all times. The staff will keep your presence here a secret. No one has any reason to look for you here or to associate the two of us. The Duchess of Sedgemere is the only one who knows I found you, and she won't speak of it except to her husband."

She nodded. She was safe, for the moment. Finally, she raised her gaze to his. "But I cannot stay here forever, and even if I could, you would not be able to keep my presence a secret for that long. The assassins will come for me, and eventually they will succeed."

"No." He said the word emphatically, bracing his legs apart as though he might take them on himself. "I won't allow any harm to come to you. I give you my word. My vow."

"How very noble." She didn't intend for the sarcasm to trickle out, but it had.

"You don't believe me?"

"Forgive me. I don't believe in anyone right now. You see, in order for the *reavlutionnaire* to carry out the attack they did, they must have had help. How else would they know how to enter the palace? How would they have found the royal chambers so quickly? My parents were dead before they had a chance to escape to the safe room. The *reavlutionnaire* knew where to find them."

"Is that how you escaped? A safe room?"

She nodded. "I was the only member of my family to reach it and only because I happened to be awake when the attack began and the alarm sounded. But the alarm was late, too late to save anyone else."

"Members of the royal court must have assisted the revolutionaries, been part of the insurgency."

"Yes. Men and women I trusted. People I knew, no doubt. So you must forgive me if I do not trust you."

"I do forgive you. Anyone who has been through what you have would feel the same. In time, you will trust again."

That was true, but he gave her too much credit. She had always seen the worst in people, never the best, even before the revolution.

"In time, I hope you can come to trust me. I have vowed to protect you, and I always honor my vows."

"Why do you make such a vow to me? Because, as you said before, you are a gentleman?"

"Yes, and because I have fond memories of Glynaven, fond memories of your family. They were very generous when I visited the court. I want to do something to honor their memory."

If he spoke the truth, he was an amazing man. If she was to believe what he said, believe anyone could be so selfless, then he was a man she must learn to trust.

He stepped closer to the bed, and their knees almost touched. "I know you don't trust me yet, but I hope you will give me the benefit of the doubt when I say we cannot travel to London yet."

She jerked back, her gaze flicking from their knees to his face. "Why?"

"Because I must appeal to the Regent personally. Even then I have no reason to believe he will make any effort to help you. He is not a man known for doing anything that does not benefit him."

*I must appeal to the Regent.*

He had not said *you* had not said *we*. It was the speech of a champion. *Her* champion.

"We can do that in person. I will appeal to the man directly."

"No. Too dangerous." The duke took her hand. His was large and warm, while hers was cold and shaking slightly. She wanted to withdraw it so he would not know she shook so, but she couldn't seem to force herself away from his heat.

"If you go to court and appeal to Prinny, we can no longer keep your presence a secret. You will be an easy target for the assassins."

"I will ask the prince to offer me protection and asylum."

The duke squeezed her hand. "And he will do so out of the kindness of his heart?" Wyndover shook his head. "He will tell you no because it's not politically expedient to protect you. England wants no part of this civil war."

"It is not a civil war! It's an insurrection!"

"Be that as it may, we did not intervene when France lopped off the heads of most of its nobility, and we will not intervene now. Prinny will want to appear neutral as the revolutionaries have some ties with Spain and Morocco. We need those countries as allies."

Anger bubbled to the surface. She knew what he was not saying. Knew money and trade were at the bottom of this.

"And Glynaven is to be sacrificed so you might keep your shipping lanes open and your ships from harassment?"

"There's the temper I remember," he said with a smile in his voice. His expression remained sober, though. "I don't say it's the correct thing to do. I merely state facts. You have nothing to bargain with, nothing to sway the Regent to your side."

She began to argue, but he put a finger over her lips.

"Let me finish and then you may rail at me all you like." The finger slid down, and despite the tingles it caused to course through her, she did not press her lips together.

"If you go to Town and approach the prince you have little chance of success and you expose yourself to danger. What I propose is writing to His Highness and gaining his support in absentia. One of my neighbors, the Duke of Stoke Teversault, always holds a ball this time of year. He and the regent are old friends, and the prince always attends the ball. We arrange to speak with the prince at Teversault. The Regent will be in good spirits and that coupled with my persuasive letter gives us the best chance I can think to assure your petition will meet with success."

The plan made sense. She was infinitely safer here, under the duke's protection than she would be without a protector at court. That was, if the duke could really control his staff and keep her presence a secret.

"There is one problem you have not considered," she said.

He arched a brow.

"Whether I am here or in London, I still have nothing to bargain with, nothing to offer the prince to induce him to support my petition for protection and asylum."

"I wouldn't say that. There are those in the prince's inner circle who might be willing to persuade him...for a price." He allowed the words to hang in the air for a long moment.

He was intimating she might become a powerful man's mistress. The very thought of sharing the bed of a man simply for gain made her ill. Was she really reduced to a state where she had nothing to offer but her body?

"But if that sort of arrangement is not to your taste, perhaps you might allow me to bargain for you."

"What can you bargain?"

"The prince needs an advocate for several bills he would propose in Parliament. I can offer to support those. If that is not enough, there's always the promise of money."

"I cannot allow you to pay for my safety."

"You could consider it a loan."

"When I have no possible way of ever repaying you?"

"Then it's a gift. Surely in your royal capacity, you have been given many gifts."

She had. And he was right that she'd never felt the need to repay the giver, although favors were certainly implied and even expected. For the first time, she did feel some obligation and a sense of duty. Wyndover owed her nothing and seemed to expect nothing in return. The more he offered her, the more indebted she felt.

Which was ridiculous. She should accept his generosity and cease questioning it. From the statements he'd made in the carriage, she could surmise he had been infatuated with her at one point. He might still be infatuated with her. He still wanted her—not that he offered assistance because he hoped to bed her in return. She knew better than to even suggest such a thing now.

But perhaps this was a means of courting her. Courting her? Did he want her for his duchess? She could not imagine why. A duchess with assassins after her would make a very poor duchess indeed.

Or perhaps he thought to seduce her…

Or perhaps he was just a kind man who wanted to help her.

Why was that so difficult to believe?

Because she'd never known kind men or women, only those who grabbed and grasped at every morsel of power they could. In the royal court of Glynaven, nothing had been free and everyone wanted something.

She did not think England was so very different. And so she would wait and watch.

"Very well, I accept your gift."

He seemed to be waiting for her to say more. When she didn't, he shook his head as though chiding himself.

"You're welcome."

He'd wanted her to thank him. Of course. She should have realized.

"If you are feeling better, I will take my leave."

Her fingers tightened on his hand. She'd be alone again with the sightless eyes. She forced her grip to loosen. She was a princess, not a frightened child, and she could hardly keep the man from his rest because she did not want to be alone.

"Good night then."

He bent and she drew back instinctively. He caught her chin with two fingers. "It's not that sort of kiss, Your Highness."

She stilled at the soft flutter of his breath whispered across her cheek. And then very slowly he dipped his mouth and brushed his lips over her temple. She closed her eyes, her heart swelling at the sweetness of the gesture. It thudded hard in anticipation when his lips trailed down and kissed her cheek. She wanted to turn her head, to meet his lips with hers. If she kissed him, took him to bed, she would not have to be alone, would not have to face those sightless eyes.

Instead, she held very still, and his lips kissed the corner of her mouth. He smelled of wine and bread and the spices that had been in the broth he'd had sent for her dinner. He smelled delicious.

Desire flooded her body with heat. It had been months and months since she'd even thought about a man in that way, and the sensation surprised her. She didn't act on it, though.

She knew he would refuse her, that his honor would compel him not to touch her. But that wasn't the only reason she resisted. This was a man of honor and principle, not some rake intent on seduction. If she bedded him, it would mean something to him and, she suspected, to her.

Best for both of them if they remained acquaintances.

But as he drew back and lifted the lamp, carrying it to the door, she knew remaining just an acquaintance would be far more difficult than she had anticipated.

# Chapter Five

She was still the most fascinating woman he'd ever known, Nathan
thought the next morning as he watched her walk in the gardens.
Like her, the flowers were in full bloom, resplendent with blossoms
in purple, pink, red, and white.

And yet, in her ugly grey dress with a hideous white collar,
she was more beautiful than all of them. The dress was too long for
her, even though he supposed one of the younger maids had given it
on loan. Vivienne had to hold them hem off the ground as she made
her way through the paths his gardeners tended. Nathan imagined
they would be thrilled someone was enjoying the garden, since he
never took the time to visit it. He had a perfect view of it from his
bedchamber window, where he stood now. But he never actually
stepped foot into it.

He never had time. Too much to do.

Even today was full of correspondence to answer and that most-important letter to the regent on Vivienne's behalf. He'd spent most of the night pondering what to offer the prince, what might sway the regent to offer Vivienne and any other refugees from Glynaven his royal protection.

Nathan could think of nothing enticing enough until he had hit upon the idea of a ship-of-the-line. Those were ridiculously expensive to build. He would offer to build one for the prince—no, he would build three. The expense would make a dent in his fortune but would not deplete it. If he managed his estates well—and he always managed his estates well—he could replace the funds in a decade or so.

Vivienne was worth that much to him and more.

It occurred to him as he made his way out of his room and toward the garden—the garden he never visited—that he intended to marry her. He had no reason to think she would agree. She hadn't been in love with him eight years ago when he'd first met her, and she didn't appear to have fallen in love with him last night.

But the truth was, he was still in love with her. He'd never fallen out of love with her. That was why he'd resisted marriage all these years, despite his mother's proddings and reminders about *that American cousin*. He'd told his mother he hadn't met a woman who could do honor to the title she'd held for so long, and when practically every fourth debutante he met fainted at his feet, that was not wholly a lie.

On the other hand, there were many very lovely, very acceptable ladies who did not faint at his feet. They might sway a little, but they showed promising fortitude.

And yet he'd tarried. Because he still wanted Vivienne. If anyone had asked him why he did not marry two days ago, Vivienne would not have crossed his mind. He didn't think of her daily, hadn't known she was the reason he put off the leg-shackling.

Until he saw her again. And then he'd known he wanted her for his duchess. Seeing her last night, sitting on that bed, her fragile shoulders hunched, her small body shaking with fear—he'd wanted her for his wife. When she'd patted the space beside her on the bed, he hadn't refused the invitation out of propriety, although that was a consideration, he'd refused it because he would not have been able to resist wrapping his arms around her and stripping that sheet away.

The sight of her bare shoulders, her small pink feet, her long dark hair falling down her back in slightly damp waves had fired his blood. And those green eyes set with determination and filled with pain. He wanted to wipe that pain away, make her eyes dark and unfocused with passion.

He shouldn't have kissed her. He'd been able to keep the kiss innocent, but it had made him want more. The feel of her soft lips on his, even if only a corner of them, made him wonder what her mouth would feel like under his.

Nathan's thoughts had occupied him all the way to the door leading to the garden, and now he paused with a hand on the knob.

He had to tamp down his lust. Somehow he had to make her fall in love with him. What could he do, could he say to engage her affections? Poetry?

He didn't know any poetry.

Flowers?

The garden was full of them.

Money? Title? She didn't want his money and had a more prestigious title than he could ever give her.

The one thing she wanted was the one thing he could not give her. No one could give her—her family back.

He stepped out the door and was immediately enveloped in the scent of flowers and soil. Bees buzzed and birds chirped and somewhere nearby one of his servants shouted.

"Dilly, where's that water I asked for?"

Nathan headed toward the section of the garden where he'd last seen Vivienne and was surprised when she stepped out before him.

"I heard you coming," she said. Her eyes were wide, and she looked a little pale.

"You thought I was someone else." He looked pointedly at her hand, where she clutched pruning shears.

She dropped them with a pretty blush that brought the color back to her skin and made her radiant. "I suppose I am a bit jumpy lately."

"Do you mind if I walk with you?"

"Of course not, but I don't wish to keep you from your duties."

"I have none at the moment." That was a lie. He always had duties. At the moment, none of them seemed to matter.

She placed her hand in the crook of his arm, and they walked in silence for a few moments. "My sister would have loved this garden," she said after some time.

"Which one?" he asked.

"Berangaria. She loved gardening."

"I remember that. She was known for her prize roses."

Vivienne nodded.

"Your sister Angelique was quite the musician."

"Did she play when you visited?" She titled her head up to look at him, her green eyes vivid in the morning light. He realized she had no bonnet, no gloves, but she did not seem concerned.

"She played several times and sang as well. She had the voice of…" He trailed off. "A songbird. What is a bird with a lovely song?"

"The lark?"

"Yes. I'm no poet."

"I am glad. Besides, with that face, I imagine you never needed to learn any poetry."

He waved a hand. His good looks were his least favorite topic of conversation.

"And your brother was known for his horsemanship. He gave me a tour of the stables. Quite impressive."

"Lucien never met a horse he didn't like." Her smile wobbled.

Nathan paused. "Forgive me. Does talking about them upset you?"

She shook her head. "No. I am glad to talk about them, remember them. My life has been a nightmare. Talking about them reminds me what it was like when my life was normal."

He gestured to a stone bench, took a seat beside her. "It will never be like it was, I'm afraid."

"No. It won't. And I will never forget—"

He put his hand over hers. "Tell me."

She shook her head. "You don't want to hear it. I will give you nightmares."

"Doubtful. I rarely dream of anything except account books and columns of numbers."

When she remained silent, he brought her hand to his lips, kissed it.

She looked at him, her eyes wary. She still didn't trust him, perhaps she never would. She might not be capable of trust.

"Talking about it might help," he said.

She nodded, released his hand and looked down at her skirts.

"What did you see?" he murmured. "What plagues you?"

"Death." Her voice was quiet, little more than a whisper. "The stench of it, the sticky feel of it beneath my bare feet, the sight of it. Masson told me not to look, and I tried. I tried. But I saw some of them, and...and..."

He heard the catch in her throat and felt the way she tensed.

"Have you ever seen death?"

"Once," he said. "I was the second at a duel. The men were supposed to shoot into the air. My friend did so but the other man did not. The ball ripped a hole in his chest, and he died on the field. Bloody, awful way to die, and there was nothing I or the physician present could do to save him."

He hadn't thought about the night in a very long time. He'd not even been twenty, and he'd thought a duel a splendid diversion. He couldn't even remember what Edmund had done to earn a glove flicked at his face. Nathan had only known he had not hesitated when his friend asked him to stand second.

His mother had not chastised him when rumor spread that he was there. She'd reminded him dueling was illegal, but he'd expected her to be much harsher. When he asked her about it later, she told him he'd been punished enough, having to watch his friend die.

Whatever crimes Vivienne had perpetrated, she had paid for.

She sighed, her body seeming to relax and to lean into his. His words had the effect of calming her, and he could be grateful for that much.

"So much death. I could not avoid it. And then there was my mother..." She paused and swallowed.

Nathan put his arm around her. "You don't have to say it."

She nodded. "I saw her in the corridor outside the safe room. She'd been trying to escape to safety. She'd been so close."

Her voice was thick with emotion, but she didn't cry. He wondered if princesses had lessons in retaining their dignity no matter the situation.

He pulled her closer, and she laid her head on his shoulder. Nathan hoped none of the servants were observing them. He did not want talk about Vivienne circulating. He trusted his staff to a point, but the more plentiful the gossip, the harder to keep it contained.

"That's not the worst part," she murmured, her voice so quiet he could barely hear her. "That's not the stuff of nightmares."

"What is the stuff of nightmares then?" He could not imagine anything worse than seeing your own mother murdered.

"The eyes." Her body shuddered. "When I try to sleep, I see all those sightless eyes staring at me. "So many pairs of eyes and so many colors—brown, blue, green, hazel. All dead. I might have been another pair of sightless eyes. I feel as though I should be."

She straightened and looked at him. Nathan wished there was something, anything he could say to ease her pain.

"Why should I be alive when so many were murdered? What did the kitchen maid ever do? The laundress? If someone is to pay for the crimes the *reavlutionnaire* accuse us of, it should have been me."

"Are you guilty of the crimes?"

"Of the excesses? Probably to some extent. Of making secret treaties and imprisoning innocent people? No."

"Your death would not have saved any of the innocents." He rose and pulled her to her feet. "Your life will ensure they are remembered."

"I hadn't thought of that. There *is* more to you than a pretty face."

He lifted her hand, kissed it. "Much more."

Nathan spent the afternoon in his library, crafting the letter he hoped would sway the Prince Regent to offer British protection for the fugitive princess from Glynaven. When he'd finished, he sent one of his grooms to London, although the prince might very well have removed to Brighton or Bath now that the Season was over.

Nathan had other work to attend to throughout the afternoon, but his mind continued to wander to the princess. He'd known she was beautiful, known she was intelligent, but the fact she'd escaped the slaughter—there was no other term for it, not in his mind—at the Glynaven palace and then made her way through the English countryside alone made her far more resourceful than he would have believed. She had inner strength as well. She couldn't stop the nightmares that plagued her sleep, but she had not uttered a tear or lost her composure once in the garden when recounting the horrors she'd seen.

He knew hundreds of women and not one could hold a candle to her.

There was a small hitch, of course. He needed a duchess, and the difference between those hundreds of women and Princess Vivienne was that the other women were literally swooning to be his duchess. Vivienne had all but told him he was far too pretty for her taste.

Well, he couldn't do a bloody thing about his looks, but he would show her he was much more than a handsome face.

"Chapple!" he bellowed, even though he had a bell pull within reach. There was something quite satisfying about bellowing for Chapple. Perhaps it was the way the butler burst into the room, eyes wide with concern.

"What is it, Your Grace?"

"Do you have it, Chapple?"

"Have what, Your Grace?" the butler panted.

"The item we discussed. The gift for the...Lady Vivienne."

"It will be delivered tonight, Your Grace."

"Good." He'd present the surprise to her tomorrow. "Tell Fletcher I'll dress for dinner now." He started toward the entry hall, Chapple following at his heels. "Lady Vivienne is aware she is expected at dinner?"

"I think so, Your Grace. I do not think she will be able to dress for the occasion, however, as she only has one dress at present."

Good point. "Then I won't change either. We will have an informal dinner. Tell Cook."

"One other matter, Your Grace."

"What is it?"

"The Duke of Stoke Teversault sent a message inquiring as to whether Wyndover Park will field an oarsman in the Dukeries Cup this year."

Damn it. Nathan had forgotten all about the annual scull race held on the serpentine lake at Teversault. At Sedgemere's house party, Lady Linton had mentioned her brother would be rowing for The Chimneys this year and William Bessett would row for Teversault. Nathan was a mediocre oarsman and he had no brothers or cousins to enter. Wyndover Park was not one of the Dukeries, but Stoke Teversault always extended the courtesy of an invitation. Nathan might have asked a friend, as he had in the past, but he did not want endanger Vivienne by inviting guests to his estate.

"Reply that Wyndover Park forfeits this year, and thank the Duke of Stoke Teversault for his courtesy."

"I beg your pardon, Your Grace." The lines around Chapple's mouth deepened with disapproval. Chapple, like all the servants, enjoyed watching the race, especially those years when the Wyndover family fielded an oarsman.

"You heard me, Chapple."

"Of course, Your Grace," Chapple said with a labored sigh.

*\*\*\**

Vivienne was grateful for the distraction of dinner. She'd spent most of the day walking the grounds and learning her way around

Wyndover Park. She might have liked to read a book, but the duke was in the library. She did not want to disturb him.

That wasn't entirely true. It wasn't that she cared so much if she disturbed him, but she didn't want to be alone with him. The way he'd held her in the garden, kissed her last night—both gestures had been sweet and innocent. The trouble was, she would have liked more of the same, only not quite so sweet and definitely not innocent.

She didn't know what was wrong with her.

She had never been free with her favors, and she had never desired a man like the Duke of Wyndover. *Ne rien!* She didn't even know his given name. It was assuredly something very pretty, like William or Charles. A pretty name to go with his pretty face.

"There you go, my lady," said the maid. The middle-aged woman had been abruptly promoted to lady's maid and tasked with styling Vivienne's hair. "You look lovely, if I do say so myself."

"It will do, O'Connell."

She did look lovely—not as pretty as the duke, but then that bar was much too high.

"Not much we can do with yer dress. It's clean, and His Grace did say he would not dress for dinner."

"Very accommodating of him," Vivienne answered, watching in the mirror as the maid fussed with the hair styling accouterment. "Does he host many dinner parties?"

"Oh, yes, my lady." O'Connell, who was tall with strawberry blond hair tucked in a cap, nodded. "Here and in

London. I travel back and forth with the family. Not all of the staff does, you see."

Vivienne nodded, understanding the maid saw this as a mark of honor.

"He hosts dozens and dozens of dinner parties, balls, and the like. He's the Duke of Wyndover."

Obviously, the maid thought that last statement explained all.

"Who plays hostess? He has no duchess." Oh, God. He wasn't married, was he? She hadn't considered that he might be married. Perhaps that was the reason he'd been so chaste in his dealings with her.

"No, my lady. Not yet. His mother plays hostess. The duchess is in Bath at present. Of course, if she hears you are here, she'll be back in an instant." O'Connell's brown eyes widened. "Not that she'll hear. We're all to remain mum on the subject."

She ought to give Wyndover more credit. "Why would she return so quickly?"

"Because she wants the duke to marry, of course. He's an only child. The duchess thought she'd never conceive and then fifteen years after she and the late duke wed—God rest his soul— here come the current duke. I wasn't with the family then, but to hear Chapple tell it, there was much rejoicing that day."

"So the duke needs an heir."

"If he doesn't produce one, the title passes to"—she lowered her voice—"an *American.*"

"Heavens." Vivienne barely suppressed a smile. Glynaven was on good terms with the United States of America, but she understood England's ambiguity toward their former colony.

"Why hasn't he married yet?" Vivienne asked more to herself than O'Connell as she didn't expect a servant to possess that information. "Surely he must meet dozens of eligible ladies at all of these family gatherings."

She'd never met the Duchess of Wyndover, but if the woman was anything like her own mother, the duke's house had been full of eligible, acceptable ladies.

"Oh, yes, but none of the ladies were like you."

Vivienne turned on the stool to face the maid directly. "What do you mean?"

"I mean no disrespect, my lady!" O'Connell held her hands up. "It's a compliment. You don't swoon when you're with him. We all thought maybe he planned to make you his duchess."

Vivienne blinked. "I don't understand. Women swoon when they're with the duke?"

"All the time, my lady." O'Connell pushed one of her loose strands of hair back under her cap. "I can hardly blame them. I mean, look at the man. I nearly swooned when I first saw him. But that was from a distance, and Mrs. Patton—she's the housekeeper—pinched me and told me if I dared faint I'd lose my position. Now I keep my eyes down when he's near." She pushed at her hair again. "If I don't look at him directly, I don't feel quite so dizzy."

Oh, this was too much. It was a wonder the man did not have the arrogance of a king. With women falling at his feet, he should have thought himself God's gift to the fairer sex. She liked him more because he'd never acted as such when he was near her. In fact, he seemed to prefer to avoid discussing his good looks.

"This has all been very interesting, O'Connell." She rose, hating the plain dress she wore and knowing she should be grateful for it.

"It wasn't gossip," O'Connell said hastily. "Mrs. Patton doesn't tolerate gossip."

"Definitely not gossip to state facts." She winked, and the maid's shoulders relaxed. Vivienne liked O'Connell. Her lady's maid at Glynaven palace had been tight-lipped and always frowning. Vivienne's hair was never tidy, her dresses too wrinkled, and she hadn't had a tender hand with a brush.

Poor Hortense was probably dead now, and Vivienne did not want to think ill of the dead, but if she ever had another lady's maid, she'd want someone like O'Connell.

She wondered if she should meet the duke in the drawing room and then decided since the dinner was informal, he would probably be waiting for her in the dining room. Thanks to her explorations earlier that day, she knew precisely where to go.

When she entered, he stood at the far side of the table, hands in his pockets, gaze on a painting on the wall across from him. For a moment she understood why women swooned. He was arrestingly handsome. All the golden hair shining in the firelight, those stunning eyes, that square jaw and chiseled cheeks.

She didn't know what he looked like underneath his clothing, but he looked very, very good in it. He was all long, lean lines and firm muscles.

She moved inside the dining room, and his gaze shifted and collided with hers. She felt a jolt when he looked at her, when all of that male beauty focused on her and her alone.

He smiled, a genuine smile that somehow made him even more attractive, although less imposing.

"You found it." He crossed to her, took her hand and kissed her knuckles. He looked up at her, and his eyes darkened. "You look beautiful."

She almost laughed. *She* looked beautiful? Hardly.

"Thank you," she said. "And thank you for dinner. You didn't have to go to the trouble, but I confess I am glad you did. This room is stunning."

And it was. The long mahogany table gleamed with china and silver. Above it a chandelier glowed softly, the unusual crystal drops hanging from each sconce making a sort of rainbow on the white-paneled walls. Red roses in short arrangements sat on either end of the sideboard and in the middle of the table. One end had been set for him and one for her.

"Tell Cook to send the first course," Wyndover said to the footman.

The man disappeared, and they were alone. Wyndover pulled out the chair beside her and gestured for her to sit. Vivienne smiled and shook her head.

"What's wrong?" His brow lowered with sudden concern.

"This seat is much too far from yours," she said. "I shall have to yell across the table."

He studied her for a long moment. "You would like to sit closer to me?"

"Is that allowed?"

"Oh, allowed and encouraged. I'll have the footman move your setting."

She waved a hand. "I may be a princess, but I know how to set a table." She moved the setting herself, and a moment later the two of them were seated beside each other, Wyndover at the head of the table and Vivienne on his right.

The footman said nothing about the altered arrangement when he returned, he merely served the soup and retreated to the corner.

Vivienne was determined to keep the conversation light, and with the servants present, she couldn't discuss Glynaven or her circumstances. She steered the conversation toward music and literature, her favorites, and Wyndover proved capable of speaking intelligently on both subjects.

He also proved a skilled conversationalist as he directed the talk toward traveling and the customs of various countries he'd visited. As she'd visited many of the same, she could add easily and with great pleasure to the subject.

They had a great deal in common, and when dinner ended, Vivienne was almost surprised to find the jasmine ice before her. They must have talked for hours, and it had seemed no time at all.

She'd drunk a little bit too much wine as the servants had filled her glass after each sip. Her head swam pleasantly, and though Wyndover was still as handsome as ever when she looked at him, she saw more than the perfect features now.

She saw the man.

And she liked what she saw.

"Why are you looking at me like that?" he asked.

She rose a bit unsteadily. "I suppose it is because I've had a wonderful evening, and I didn't expect it."

He rose as well, taking her elbow. He must have thought to steady her, but she was not that intoxicated.

"What sort of evening did you expect?"

She shrugged, a gesture she would only make when in her cups as she'd been told at least a thousand times that princesses did not shrug.

"The sort where you wax poetic on the leek soup and exclaim at the sauce on the potatoes."

His mouth turned up at the corner. It was a very nice mouth. She wanted to kiss it, but that would probably shock the servants. She scanned the room. No servants at the moment. They'd removed all but the ices, and were probably in the kitchen taking a moment's respite.

"I know the sort of evening you mean. I don't think either of us had anything poetic to say about the leek soup. I must say the sauce on the potatoes was quite to my liking."

She lifted her hand and placed it against his smoothly shaved cheek. "You are quite to my liking."

He didn't blink, didn't breathe.

After a long silence, he shifted slightly. "I thought I was too pretty for you."

"Oh, you're very pretty." Her fingers stroked his cheek and trailed down to his jaw. "But I shan't be swooning, if that is your concern."

He grasped her hand. "Who told you?"

"It's common knowledge, Duke. What is your Christian name, by the way?"

"Nathan. Why?"

"I like to know a man's name before I kiss him."

He still held her wrist in his hand, and when she leaned in to kiss him, he hesitated just for a moment. Then he dropped her hand and bent as her arms circled his neck and she pulled his mouth to hers.

## Chapter Six

She tasted of jasmine ices and the sweet wine they'd drank together. She tasted better than he could imagine. And the feel of her...

He dared not put his arms around her because he couldn't trust himself to behave. She'd pressed her body to him, her lush breasts pushing against his chest, her long, aristocratic fingers in his hair. Her mouth was gentle and full and her kisses very, very thorough. He'd expected the kiss to be sloppy. But she wasn't foxed, or if she was, she was very good at disguising the fact.

She drew back, looked up at him. Her green eyes were so large they filled his vision.

"Put your arms around me. Or—" She leaned back. "Would you rather I stop?"

"God, no. Don't stop."

He put his hands on her waist, pulled her body back against his. This time he noted the heat of her. Such a small thing to generate so much heat. He cupped her face with his hands, running his thumbs over her delicate cheekbones, then brushing his lips over hers. Her mouth parted slightly, and he took her plump lower lip in a kiss, nipping it gently.

She moaned, her hands roaming his back. Nathan was aware the servants might return at any moment. They should stop kissing, but he couldn't seem to abandon her mouth. Every touch of his lips to hers made him want more. Finally, when she opened for him, where their tongues touched and tangled and mated, he swore he could hear music. He'd wanted this so long, he hadn't thought the reality could live up to his imaginings. His very detailed imaginings.

But her lips were plumper, her mouth sweeter, the stroke of her tongue more tantalizing than he could have ever fantasized. And when her hands slid down to his buttocks, he had to grip the edge of the table to keep from ravishing her then and there.

He had never wanted a woman, never wanted anything as much as he wanted her in that instant.

"Take me to bed," she whispered, her velvet cheek brushing against his.

Nathan clutched the table tighter, struggling for control.

"No."

She looked up at him, a brow arched. "You don't want me?"

"Oh, I want you. In another moment I shall crack this table with the force of my *want*."

She looked at his hand clenching the table then back at his eyes. "I've done something wrong. I've been too forward. I forget you English prefer your women more coy."

"No." He gripped her shoulders. "I like you exactly as you are. But if I take you"—he lowered his voice in case the servants were about—"if I take you to bed tonight, I will be taking advantage of your intoxicated state."

"I am not so intoxicated."

"Be that as it may, I prefer to give you time to reconsider."

"Very noble of you. If I do not reconsider?"

"Then you should know I want more than a night or two of bedsport with you."

"You want my affections?"

He touched her throat and trailed down to the center of her chest and that godawful collar. He forced himself to stop there, not to stray to the swells of her breasts. "I want your heart."

Vivienne took a shaky breath. "Perhaps time to consider is warranted."

She stepped back and out of his arms. Immediately, she wrapped her own arms around her body. Nathan could not tell if it was a protective gesture or one of thwarted longing.

"Will you ride with me in the morning? There's something I want to show you."

"Yes. I'd like that. I haven't ridden since…before."

He bowed. "Then I bid you goodnight. I will see you at the stables in the morning."

As difficult as it was to walk away from her, he accomplished it, not pausing until he reached his room. In his bedchamber, he leaned against the door and closed his eyes.

"Shall I leave you, Your Grace?" Fletcher asked, coming out of the dressing room. Nathan opened his eyes to study the tall, thin man soberly dressed in black. Fletcher and Nathan were close in age, but Fletcher always seemed a good deal older. He already showed streaks of gray in his dark hair, and his face had a pinched look.

"Yes. No. I don't know." Nathan pushed away from the door. "She'll refuse me, Fletcher." Nathan paced his room. "I can hardly blame her. She doesn't even know me. I must be daft to think of asking her to marry me."

Fletcher clasped his hands behind his back. "Lady Vivienne is the object of your affection, I take it."

"Damn it, Fletcher. You were with me when I toured the Continent. You know she's not *Lady* Vivienne."

"I also know the princess could do far worse than you, Your Grace."

Nathan gave the man a wan smile. "I'm not paying you enough, Fletcher."

"I would not decline higher wages, but I am paid as well if not better than my counterparts. I am not flattering you, Your Grace. I honestly believe the princess would be lucky to have you. From what I know of her, *you* would be fortunate to marry her. She is intelligent, accomplished, and politically astute."

"All that and more."

"Without question."

Nathan dropped into a chair and put his face in his hands. "You make it sound so logical and reasonable, when this marriage business is anything but. What if she refuses me?"

"Then you ask someone else, Your Grace."

Nathan laughed and pushed his fingers against his tired eyes. "I don't want someone else."

"Then make certain she says yes."

\*\*\*

The morning dawned cloudy but dry, and Vivienne was prompt. He'd had a mare saddled for her, one of the more spirited horses, and she approved the animal and mounted with little assistance. She wore one of the duchess's out of fashion riding habits that O'Connell and another maid had stayed up all night to alter. It was a lovely blue with gold piping, and as soon as she climbed on her mount, she felt right at home.

Nathan rode his favorite gelding. Patch was known as such because he had a white patch on his chest. Nathan's mother had named the horse, and Nathan hadn't changed it.

He and Vivienne rode to the west. Vivienne had a good seat and when he was certain she could keep up, Nathan gave Patch his head. The two of them galloped for a mile or so, enjoying the morning and the silence broken only by the call of birdsong. At least Nathan should have been enjoying it. Instead he was thinking of the instructions he'd given to Chapple. He had to keep Vivienne away from Wyndover Park long enough for Chapple to arrange everything just so.

"What is over there?" Vivienne asked, pointing toward one of his tenant's lands.

"That's the Holland's farm, I believe."

Nathan studied the faint spiral of smoke coming from the farm and turned Patch in that direction. "Wait here."

A moment later, he neared the tenant's cottage and Vivienne was right behind him. He wasn't surprised. He doubted she was very used to following orders.

"There's where the smoke came from."

A circle of stones ringed still smoldering chunks of wood. The fire looked to have been hastily put out and not very thoroughly. Nathan jumped down and inspected the site then knocked on the tenant's door.

No one answered.

He walked back to Patch and was about to mount when he head hoof beats.

"Who is that?" Vivienne asked.

"My steward."

The man removed his hat and dismounted as soon as he arrived. "Your Grace. My lady. I didn't expect to see you here." Mr. Husselbee was tanned and freckled from so much time outdoors. He had an easy smile and a friendly face. In short, he was a man who could collect rents and still find a way to remain on good terms with the tenants.

"We saw the smoke," Nathan explained with a wave of his hand.

Husselbee frowned and examined the site himself. Hands on hips, he turned back to the duke. "The Hollands are away for a fortnight. Mrs. Holland is from Dorset, and her sister wrote to say her mother was ill. I told Holland I'd feed the livestock and check on the farm while they were away."

"Then who built this fire?"

Husselbee shook his head. "I don't know. Vagrants, I suspect. I'll make a thorough tour of the ducal land after I tend to the Holland's livestock. If I find anyone, I'll run them off with a strict warning."

"Very good, sir." Nathan mounted again. "Come by the house after your tour and give me a full update."

"Yes, Your Grace."

When they were away, Vivienne spurred her horse and rode beside him. "I don't like it."

Nathan raised a brow. "Vagrants? You should know that sort of thing is common enough. My game wardens frequently have to arrest poachers. I let them go with a warning. Times are hard. People are hungry."

Vivienne studied him, her green eyes sparkling in diffuse morning light. "That's very kind of you. I do know poachers and vagrants are common. I suppose I feared the campsite might have housed the Glennish assassins."

He saw the flash of fear in her eyes before she lowered them.

Nathan reached over and grasped her hand. "They can't have found you here. No one knows where you are. You're safe. I promised I would protect you, and I will."

She raised her gaze to his again. "I believe you."

He released her hand, and they rode in silence again for a time.

"Shall we stop there and walk a bit?" she asked, indicating a stream that flowed along the back of his property. He'd had it stocked with trout, even though he didn't enjoy fishing.

At the stream, the horses drank and grazed while he and Vivienne walked the banks. Finally, they came to a shady spot where the stream widened into a small pond. It was not quite the size of the Sedgemere's pond, and certainly not big enough for boating, but he'd swum in it as a boy and had a jolly time playing pirate.

Under a willow tree, Vivienne turned to him. "Should we continue our conversation from last night?"

Nathan's heart galloped, although he'd been trying to form the right words all morning. "I...yes," he managed weakly and swore silently at his idiocy. She would be right to refuse him. Sedgemere had been right about him. He'd relied too much on his good looks and had no skill when it came to wooing women. Why the devil hadn't he memorized some bloody Byron?

"You said last night, you wanted more than just my body and my affections."

Had he said that? Good God. He had been bold after the wine and her kisses.

"You want my heart."

"I do. I want more than a…a liaison."

"I'm not in love with you," she said, and his heart fell into his belly.

"Of course not."

"But I could fall in love with you."

His head jerked up, his gaze searching her face. She smiled.

"Oh, I could very easily fall in love with you, Nathan." Her hands slid to his shoulders. "Do I have leave to call you Nathan?"

"Call me whatever you want."

"I've never known a man like you," she said.

He winced. "Is this about my face again."

She closed her eyes and shook her head. "No. This is about how kind and generous and thoughtful you are."

"In the interest of full disclosure, not all of my actions toward you have been wholly unselfish."

She laughed. "Thank God. I was beginning to think you were not human."

"I'm very human," he said as she pressed against him. "Exceedingly human."

"Is it enough if I say you have a corner of my heart? Is it enough if I say you could very well have all of it one day?"

"It's enough."

And it was because it was not only more than he had ever expected, but he simply couldn't resist her any longer. His body was on fire with need, and—as she'd pointed out—he was only human.

He bent his head to kiss her, pulling her hand against him. Her mouth opened for him, her lips meeting his with the same passion and same intensity. He was left with no question as to what she wanted from him. He hadn't imagined he would lie with her outdoors—very well, he'd actually imagined lying with her everywhere, but he hadn't *expected* to lie with her outdoors—but he would not argue the point.

He stripped off his coat, dropped it under the tree and allowed his hands to travel down her slim back. He cupped her bottom, brought her hips into contact with his erection. She moaned and rocked against him. Her own hands explored him—his back, his chest, his buttocks, his cock.

When she slid her hand over the fall of his trousers, Nathan grabbed the trunk of the tree for support.

"Your body is as perfect as your face," she murmured when he kissed her neck. "You're hard all over."

He was hard, indisputably hard. His hands skidded over her side and up to cup her breasts. With a groan, her head fell back. Through the layers she wore, he felt her nipples pebble against his hands and wished he could see them, kiss them.

She pulled him down, settling herself on his coat. "My legs won't hold up much longer," she said, her voice husky. "You've made them wobbly and weak."

His hand slid under her skirts and up her stocking-clad leg until he reached the bare flesh of her thigh. "They feel fine to me." He kissed her again, his hand stroking her soft flesh. "Very fine."

"Don't tease me, Nathan," she murmured. "Not this time. Next time, perhaps, or the time after that. Not this time."

"I am yours to command," he answered, his hand cupping the warm, wet flesh at the juncture of her thighs.

A sigh escaped her parted lips, but her eyes—so dark now—never left his face.

He touched her, explored her gently, until she arched beneath him. Her cheeks were pink with arousal, and when he slid two fingers inside her, circled her small nub with his thumb, her eyes seemed to blur and lose focus.

"Let go, Princess," he murmured. "No one will hear you but me."

Her hips rose, and he lessened his pressure slightly. In a rush, she bowed back, a strangled cry drifting through the trees. He withdrew, studied her face. She lay with her eyes closed, chest rising and falling, cheeks stained lovely pink, and her lips plump and red.

Finally, she opened her eyes and smiled. "Nathan, do you know how to dress and undress a lady?"

He wasn't certain how to answer. He'd dressed and undressed his share, but it wasn't a subject he wished to discuss with the woman he hoped to make his wife.

"I see that you do. Good." She rose to her knees and gave him her back. "Unfasten me, will you?"

His hands fumbled at the hooks and eyes, the ties and knots, the pins and tapes. Finally, he had her out of the outer layers of clothing, and she stood in her shift.

"I don't think anyone will come this way," he said, "but I cannot be certain."

"Then I suppose I had better not stand about all day."

With a flick of her finger at the knot at her neck, the chemise came loose and slid down her body. He followed its progress hungrily. The material uncovered ripe, full breasts tipped with dark, erect nipples, a slim waist, lush hips, and plump thighs.

"You take my breath away," he whispered.

"Good." She turned and walked to the edge of the pond, her derriere as round and perfect as the rest of her. She dipped a toe in the water, let out a little shriek, then moved resolutely forward.

Finally, she'd submerged herself to just below her breasts. She turned to him, giving him a view he could have enjoyed all day.

"It's not so cold, especially once you get used to it. What are you waiting for, Duke?"

"Nothing."

He stripped off his neck cloth and pulled at his boots.

"Do hurry, Your Grace. I'm naked and wet and cold. I need you to warm me."

"I am hurrying, Your Highness. I haven't any aid, as you did."

Finally, he was as naked as she, and painfully aroused as she watched him approach.

"I should hate you," she said.

He paused, one foot in the water.

"You are the most perfect man I have ever seen. You could at least have a scar or a withered arm or some such thing to even out the face. But no. You could be a Michaelangelo."

The water was not cold, and he forced himself not to look overeager to reach her. "You act as though that is a bad thing."

He reached for her, pulling her into his arms. Her warm body was slippery and slick.

"You might have been a Botticelli," he said, kissing her neck. "You're lush and soft and—"

She wrapped her legs around him, and he blew out a breath.

"And?" she prompted.

"I can't think."

"Then don't."

Her legs wrapped around his waist, and he slid inside her quickly and more roughly than he'd intended. She didn't complain, only tightened around him and kissed him deeper.

He hands cupped her bottom, pulling her harder against him and angling her until she slid up and down in a way he knew would give her the greatest pleasure. Her eyes widened after his first few thrusts, and her breath quickened.

"You're quite good at this," she gasped as he drove into her again.

"I suppose..." He clenched his jaw and attempted to maintain control. "You will hold that against me as well."

"Not at all. This—" She shuddered and clenched around him. "For this I can forgive anything."

"Even my face?"

"Even that."

He couldn't hold on any longer, and he thrust hard into her, hoping it would be enough to bring her to climax. He felt her muscles clamp around him and the satisfaction of knowing he'd brought her pleasure again was almost as good as his own release.

Almost.

Because when they finally climbed out of the water and lay spent and sated in each other's arms, Nathan felt the one thing he had never felt with any woman ever before: certainty.

# Chapter Seven

Vivienne would have been content to lie in Nathan's arms all day if her flesh hadn't started to resemble that of a plucked goose.

"You're shivering," he said, and his words alone thawed her. He noticed everything about her, wanted to keep her warm and safe.

"I don't mind. I like it here with you."

"I like it too, but I did say I had something to show you."

She rose on her elbow, faced him. "There's more?" Her gaze slid down his body—his absolutely perfect body—and the color rose in his cheeks. He was so adorable. She wanted to have him again.

"Dress, and I'll show you."

It was easier said than done, but with his help, the tedious chore was finally accomplished. Her hair was mostly dry, as O'Connell's excellent coiffure had stayed in place. Vivienne imagined it was a bit lopsided, but she didn't particularly care. Today was the first time she'd felt any real joy or happiness since the attack on the palace.

It wasn't only Nathan's lovemaking, either. Being with him made her happy. She'd wakened long before dawn this morning, too excited about the prospect of seeing him to sleep any longer. She hadn't lied when she'd told him he had a corner of her heart. In truth, she'd been modest. He had captured it whole.

The prospect scared her. Everyone she'd loved was dead. Everyone who'd cared for her was dead, and the men seeking to kill her were still at large. She had no right to involve Nathan in this deadly game of cat and mouse. She had no right to care for him. Caring for him might just mean his death.

They rode back to the house, which looked impressive with the streaks of sunlight breaking through the clouds behind it. Nathan led her to the back, but instead of turning in the direction of the stables, he motioned toward the lawn. In the middle of the long expanse of green bordered by pink and purple flowers, she spotted three targets made of straw and painted with red circles in the middle.

A groom took her mount and handed her down, and she joined Nathan and his butler.

"Duke, I didn't know you had an interest in archery."

He smiled, the smile of a man with a secret. "I don't. I know you do." He held out a hand and the butler reached in a sack at his feet. He pulled out a quiver of arrows followed by a bow and handed them to Nathan.

"What do you think?" the duke asked.

"Very nice." She stepped closer to better appreciate the fine craftsmanship of the bow. "May I?" she asked, indicating the arrows.

"Please."

She lifted one out and nodded approval at the straight line of the shaft and the high quality of the fletching.

"For a man with little interest in archery, this is an extraordinary set."

"It's for you."

She jerked her head up, uncertain she'd heard him correctly. "Me?"

"Yours was…lost. This is a replacement."

"But this is too much." She'd never given a second thought to the cost of things before, but since the attack had left her with nothing, she'd begun to think of money more and more. That didn't stop her hand from curling around the handle of the bow. She itched to try it, to pluck the string and see if it sang.

"Go ahead," Nathan said. "These targets are for you."

A thrill of excitement raced through her. Archery had always been one of her favorite pastimes, one at which she excelled. Now she fitted the bow around her hands, took a moment to accustom herself to the weight and the feel of it. Then she pulled an arrow from the quiver and pointed it at the target on her right.

"Not that one," Nathan said.

She glanced at him over the bow.

"Start on the left."

Strange request, but she didn't argue. She shifted until she faced the new target, notched her arrow, and pulled back the string. With a satisfying *twang* the arrow soared toward the target, hitting the red center circle just to the left.

"Very good, my lady," the butler remarked.

Vivienne narrowed her eyes, calculating her error. She squared her shoulders and, facing the center target, pulled another arrow from the quiver. She made a slight modification in how she held the bow and let the arrow soar. It hit the center dead in the middle.

She allowed a small smile to curve her lips.

"If you'll excuse me, Your Grace," the butler said and started back toward the house. Vivienne hardly saw him go. She turned to the last target and positioned the bow then pulled another arrow from the quiver.

She was aware Nathan stood beside her, feet braced apart and arms crossed over his chest. He shifted slightly, and she had a moment to wonder what he was nervous about before the target consumed her focus.

She narrowed her eyes, pulled the string of the bow back, and let the arrow fly. It made a small *ping* when it hit.

"I hope I didn't break the tip," she said. Without waiting for his answer, she marched across the grass and examined the center of the target.

Something gold glittered in the filtered sunlight. Her arrow had pierced it through.

She pulled the arrow from the strawy and the small circle came with it, balanced precariously on the tip of the arrow. Vivienne's heart lurched.

It was a ring—a ring with a rather large diamond in the center surrounded by green stones she assumed must be emeralds.

She jerked around almost bumping into Nathan who had come to stand beside her. Before she could say a word, he bent to one knee.

"The ring was my mother's—not her wedding ring. She still wears that. It was a gift from my father on my birth. I always think of you when I see it because of the emeralds. They're almost as beautiful as your eyes."

"Does this mean what I think it means?" she asked, her voice shaking. Every part of her shook now—her legs, her belly, her hands.

"I want you to be my wife, my duchess. I know this may seem sudden. You don't know me very well, but it's all I've wanted for the last eight years. I never forgot you."

"I don't know what to say," she finally managed.

"You could say yes."

The look in his eyes almost melted her. She could see the love in his face, in the way he looked at her. She'd seen it in the way her father had looked at her mother. But did she feel the same or were her burgeoning feelings only infatuation or, worse, gratitude for his kindness?

"I…" she began, uncertain what she would say. At the moment, her English all but eluded her.

He held up a hand. "Or you could tell me you need more time."

When she didn't answer, he winced. "Or you could tell me no." He rose slowly, brushing the grass from his trousers. She took his hand, looked up and into his eyes, bluer even than the sky on this cloudy day.

"The answer is most definitely not *no*." She pressed the ring into his palm. "But it's not yes either. Keep this for me? I hope when I am ready, you will offer it again?"

"Of course." He stepped back, pocketing the ring in his waistcoat. The air around him was formal now, and how she wished she could bring back the easy mood of their morning.

"Thank you for the bow and arrows. I would say you have no idea how much it means to me, but it occurs to me that perhaps you do understand."

"I do," he said, and the answer seemed to encompass more than her thanks for the archery set. "Stay and practice as long as you like. I have some business to attend to."

"Oh." She had hoped they might spend more time together. "Will I see you at dinner?"

"Of course. And I've asked one of the maids to take your measurements. The housekeeper assures me she's an adequate seamstress. Perhaps in a few days you will have several more gowns. Tell the maid what fabrics you like, and they will be ordered from the town or from London, if they are not available here."

"You are too generous."

"I have more money than I can spend. A few dresses and an archery set are hardly largesse. And, as I said, I'm not entirely unselfish. I want you to fall in love with me."

With those words, he bowed and started back toward the house.

"Nathan," she called after him.

He paused and turned back to face her.

"I'm falling."

\*\*\*

The next days were filled with pleasant morning rides and scintillating dinners. Vivienne was all Nathan could want in a woman and more. He'd vowed not to take her again until after she'd agreed to be his wife, but he could hardly resist when, laughing, she pulled him into an empty stall in the stable or when she opened her bed chamber door at night and tugged him inside.

She was passionate, witty, energetic, and diverting. He'd never enjoyed himself as much as he did when he was with her.

He'd never laughed so much, talked so much, craved someone's touch so much.

It wasn't only her touch. Just the act of seeing her or hearing her voice, made his heart swell and lift.

Since the day of the proposal, he had not brought up marriage again. She knew his desires, and she would give him an answer when she was ready. In the meantime, he began to look for a response to his request from the Prince Regent. She didn't ask directly if he'd received an answer, but he often saw a hopeful look in her eyes. He shook his head when she raised her brows in question, and they waited.

One morning, about a week after the proposal, the two of them were met by Mr. Husselbee as they walked back to the house.

"Your Grace." He gave a bow. "My lady." Another bow. "I trust there have been no more signs of vagrants in the area."

"None," Nathan answered. "Did you catch the men?"

"No. I tracked them to the edge of the property and lost the trail. I think they must be long gone and someone else's problem now. The Holland family has returned and reported nothing in their house or shed was disrupted."

"Very good."

Vivienne touched his arm. "I will leave you gentlemen to discuss crops and farms and livestock. Excuse me."

Nathan watched her go then asked Husselbee to join him in the library.

Husselbee sat in the chair across from Nathan's desk and elaborated on the condition of the estate. Finally, he took a breath, let it out, then took another.

"Is something troubling you, Mr. Husselbee?"

"Yes, Your Grace. I'm not certain how to proceed. You see, ever since one of the maids ordered those fine fabrics from the town, there's been talk. Who are such fine fabrics for? I don't blame the girl, Your Grace. She didn't say anything to set tongues wagging, but you know how people are."

"Can't we say they are for my mother?"

"Not in the proportions ordered, Your Grace. Your mother is tall and—er, ample compared to Lady Vivienne."

"I see."

"And there's more talk, Your Grace. Usually when you are in residence you host some of the local gentry for dinner or a garden party. No one has been invited to visit, and you've been here almost a fortnight."

"I understand, Husselbee. Unfortunately, I don't have a solution for you at this time. Lady Vivienne has fallen into some unfortunate circumstances—through no fault of her own—and it is best if we keep her presence here a secret for the time being."

"Yes, Your Grace. I'll do my best for as long as I can."

Nathan knew that couldn't be much longer.

He went to sleep late. He'd had another engaging dinner with Vivienne, and when she'd hinted she would welcome a visit from him after the servants had gone to bed, he had politely refused.

He wanted a wife, not a mistress. Oh, he liked bedding her well enough. She was enthusiastic and imaginative. But he wanted more than bedsport. He wanted a wife, a partner, a mother for his children.

He had thought she would give him an answer by now, and there had been times he had looked at her and seen something in her eyes. He'd held his breath, certain she would ask for the ring again—the ring he kept always in his waistcoat.

But she had not asked, had not declared her love for him, and because she hesitated, so did he. He wanted to hold her in the aftermath of their lovemaking, stroke her hair, and tell her he loved her. But he didn't dare push her or pressure her to say more than she was willing.

And so he waited far longer than usual to go to bed. He'd dismissed Fletcher so his valet could rest, and Nathan did little more than shed his coat before falling into bed. He didn't even bother to toe off his boots. It wasn't the first time he'd slept in his clothes, although it was more comfortable when he was foxed.

Still, he fell into a deep, dreamless sleep, only coming awake slowly at the pinch in his neck.

He opened his eyes and stared at the man bending over him. "Don't move or I'll slit your throat."

Nathan didn't move.

"Good. Now tell me where she is, and we'll let you live."

"Where who is?" Nathan croaked.

"Princess Vivienne."

## Chapter Eight

He hadn't come to her. She'd waited, the lamp burning, her heart thudding for what seemed hours. At midnight, she realized he wouldn't come. She could hardly blame him. He wanted an answer to his proposal. He deserved an answer, and she hadn't given it.

She'd wanted to give it so many times—wanted to tell him *yes, yes, yes*. She loved him, couldn't help but love him, despite that too handsome face and perfect body.

And because she loved him she had not given him an answer. Because she loved him, she couldn't bear to put him in danger.

But perhaps the danger was over. The assassins must have given up searching for her now. They'd be expected back in Glynaven, undoubtedly had superiors to report to. Perhaps she could give Nathan the answer he wanted. The answer she wanted.

And she did not want to wait until the morning.

She climbed out of bed naked, stumbled over the bow and arrows she'd left by the bed, and found her shift on the Chinese screen. She pulled it on, considered lighting a lamp, and then decided she knew the way to his rooms well enough without it.

The moment she stepped into the corridor, she knew something was amiss. The hair rose on the back of her arms even before she saw the shadow across from his room.

Clamping a hand over her mouth, she dove back into her chamber, closing the door silently and locking it behind her.

They'd found her.

The assassins had found her.

They hadn't given up after all. They were here, and this time they would kill her.

The sightless eyes flashed in her mind again—all those eyes and the blood on the carpets, soaking into her slippers. She couldn't bear to see it again. She couldn't shoulder the guilt of bringing death to so many innocents at Wyndover Park.

She had to go. She had to flee before the assassins found her and slit her throat.

She stumbled toward the Chinese screen and the boots set neatly behind it. She did not care about a dress, but she could not run without boots. She knew that well enough. She bent to pull them on when her mind froze and even in her panicked state one word broke through: Nathan.

She couldn't leave him.

Vivienne shook her head.

He was dead. He had to be. They'd already killed him. She could only save herself now.

But her hand dropped away from the boots, and her gaze tracked to the bow and arrow near the bed. Even if he was dead, she couldn't leave him. He would have never left her. He would have given anything to keep her safe. If there was a chance he still lived, she had to go to him.

Snatching the bow and arrow in her hands, she readied an arrow and tiptoed back to the door.

Silently, she turned the lock and eased the door open. The hinges made no sound, and if she lived she would thank Mrs. Patton for that later.

Peering around the doorjamb, she saw the corridor was empty. For a moment she hoped she'd imagined the shadow and the man's form, but then she heard the low rumble of men's voices coming from Nathan's room.

Keeping against the wall, she crept down the hallway. Her heart beat so hard, her chest ached, and she was almost dizzy from the fear. As she neared the room, she heard the most terrifying sound yet—Glennish.

If she'd had any doubts before, she had none now. These were the assassins, and they had Nathan.

Alive.

She knew that because she heard him answer them. "I don't know what you're talking about," he said. "I don't know any princess."

"He lies," one of them hissed in her native tongue. "Kill him."

"Slit his throat, and we'll find her ourselves. She's here."

Nathan would die. For her.

Vivienne stepped into the doorway, arrow nocked and ready. She assessed the situation quickly. Two men were near the door and the third had a knife to Nathan's throat where he lay on the bed.

"Touch him and I'll shoot you through."

One of the men by the door jerked toward her, and she swung her bow toward him. "Don't do it," she said in Glennish. "If you know anything about me, you know I can kill all three of you before you could shout for help. If there were anyone who would help you."

She swung her bow back to the man kneeling over Nathan. "Get off him and back away slowly."

"I'll cut his throat and then yours, *princess*."

"Get off him!" she shouted, afraid to wait too much longer, knowing every moment she waited was another closer to Nathan's death.

The assassin didn't move.

God! God! God!

She didn't want to kill him. She'd never killed anyone, man or beast.

But her gaze collided with Nathan's. His eyes focused on her, still alive, still full of love. She couldn't allow him to become another of the sightless eyes that haunted her.

*Twang.*

She loosed the arrow, heard the sickening *thunk* as it struck flesh. She yanked another from her quiver just as quickly and swiveled to face the last two assassins.

\*\*\*

Nathan pushed the dead weight of the assassin off and jumped to his feet. Vivienne stood across the room, arrow trained on the two men intent on killing her. Both had drawn their knives—long, sharp weapons—Nathan had no doubt they would use on her or anyone else in their way.

He had to help her, but for the first time in his life, he felt utterly helpless. He had no weapon, no means to rescue her. She'd rescued him.

At an imperceptible signal, the assassins separated and began to circle the princess.

"Don't move," she ordered in Glennish.

The assassins ignored her. She couldn't shoot them at the same time, and if she fired at one, the other could attack. Nathan took a step toward the one closest to him. The man brandished his weapon.

"Stay back," he ordered.

"Nathan, be careful!"

He'd distracted her, and the assassins were now on either side of her. She had to pivot from one to the other in order to keep her arrow trained on them. She was fast and agile, but she couldn't hold them off forever. Nathan pressed his weight onto the balls of his feet, preparing to throw himself at one assassin, thereby removing one target. He'd probably end up dead and without an heir. The bloody American cousin would have the title.

His poor mother.

Nathan lunged just as the dressing room door opened. Nathan caught the distracted assassin about the waist, and the two tumbled to the rug. Nathan got in a good jab to the man's back before he rolled and brandished the knife in Nathan's direction.

"Let him go," Vivienne said, her voice full of command.

"I'm fine," Nathan answered. "I can take him."

The assassin jabbed at him, narrowly missing.

"Or not," Nathan muttered.

"I believe she meant me, Your Grace."

Nathan's head jerked at the sound of his valet's voice. "Fletcher!"

His valet stood in front of the other assassin, the man's knife a steel slash across his exposed neck.

"I heard a sound and thought you might require assistance, Your Grace."

Goddamn it all to hell. "Let him go!" Nathan shouted in Glennish, kicking out to prevent his own attacker from coming closer. Thank God he still had the boots on. The knife grazed his calf and would have split his skin open without the protection of the thick leather.

"Lower the arrow," the assassin holding Fletcher told Vivienne. The assassin was dark and short, holding his knife like a seasoned warrior, whereas the one Nathan fought was younger and moved with less certainty.

"Let him go," Vivienne countered.

"Shoot him, Vivienne," Nathan said, kicking at his assassin again. This time the knife did pierce his boot and the warm blood trickled down his skin.

She shook her head, her eyes never leaving the assassin's face. "Let him go. I don't want to kill you."

"I'll kill him then you," the assassin hissed. "Put down your weapon."

She hesitated and her arm wavered.

"No!" Nathan yelled. Their only chance was to kill one of the assassins. "Kill him!"

"I can't!"

The dark assassin pulled the arm with the knife back, and Fletcher closed his eyes.

\*\*\*

Vivienne closed her eyes and let go. She half-prayed the arrow would miss, though it would mean the death of an innocent man.

But she didn't miss. Of course she didn't miss. She never did.

The assassin screamed as the arrow plunged into the side of his face, the side exposed over Fletcher's shoulder. The man's knife clattered to the floor, and Fletcher went down on his knees, looking like he might fall over from the shock of it.

There was no time to help the valet, no time to render any aid to the wounded assassin writhing on the floor. He'd be dead in a moment or two. Dead because of her.

She pushed the thought aside and reached for another arrow, swung to Nathan.

But the third assassin was gone.

Nathan held his arm. Under his hand, the white sleeve of his shirt bloomed red.

"Your Grace," Fletcher wheezed. "You're hurt."

"I'm fine." He rose to his feet, looking a little unsteady but solid.

Vivienne felt unsteady too. She wanted to collapse, to cry for days, to run into his arms and bury her face in his chest. Instead, she gestured with the arrow toward the open bedchamber door.

"We have to go after him." She didn't add what she'd been thinking: before he murdered one of the innocent servants.

"Not without a weapon." Nathan pushed the dead man on his bed over and yanked the knife from his hand. "Now I'm ready. Follow me."

Without waiting for her agreement, he started forward, pausing at the door to sweep his gaze in both directions.

"Fletcher?"

"Left, Your Grace."

Nathan glanced at her over his shoulder. "Coming?"

He didn't tell her to stay. He didn't expect her to wait for him, like a helpless girl. This was her battle too, and he knew it, respected her need to end this herself.

Oh, how she loved him.

"I'm coming." She raised the arrow again and followed him into the corridor.

Nothing but shadows and the distant sound of a clock's pendulum swinging back and forth with a quiet ticking. At the first doorway, which was closed, Nathan put a finger to his lips and lifted the latch. He pushed inside, knife raised, and she followed swinging her arrow left and right. He parted the drapes, opened the tall boy against the wall, and peered under the bed.

"Empty," Nathan declared.

She moved back into the hallway and he followed.

"There's only one more room this way, a servant's closet."

"And that door?" She pointed to a doorway made to look like the wall's paneling.

"The servant's stairs. I'm betting he took those."

"I think you're right. He wants to escape."

"He wants to kill you. I don't think he's given up yet."

She agreed with him on that point as well. He started for the end of the hallway, but she grabbed his uninjured arm and pulled him back.

"Nathan."

He gave her an impatient glance then looked over his shoulder at the door. Vivienne lowered her weapon and took his face in her hands. That earned her his full attention.

"Just in case I don't have another opportunity, I wanted to tell you I love you."

"You will have another opportunity. But I love you too."

She smiled. She couldn't contain the burst of joy that raced through her. "Do you have the ring?"

"What?"

He must think her mad, and perhaps she was. This was no time to discuss marriage, and yet, she'd seen how quickly life as one knew it could come to a crashing end. Now might be the only chance she ever had.

"Your mother's emerald ring?"

He stared at her for a long moment then his hand passed over the pocket of his waistcoat. "Are you saying you'll marry me?"

"Yes. I was coming to tell you when I interrupted that tete-a-tete in your room."

"I much prefer your company at any rate." He pulled the ring from his waistcoat. "I don't have time to do this properly."

She waved his protest away. "Put it on my finger. That's as proper as I need or want."

He took her hand, slid the ring on her finger clumsily.

She kissed him quickly, ran her thumb over the unfamiliar piece of jewelry on her hand.

"Now, let's go catch an assassin," she said.

\*\*\*

He would die. She'd finally told him she loved him, finally agreed to be his wife, his duchess, and now he was off to his death. Life was full of injustice. Nathan just hadn't ever had so much of it thrown his direction.

He led her down the servant's stairwell, emerging silently onto the house's ground floor. Short corridor leading to the expansive vestibule in front of him, door to his library, which led to a parlor on his left. Door to the music room, which opened to a large sitting room on his right. The dining room was on the other side of the vestibule.

"I'll take this side, you take that," Vivienne said.

"Hell, no. Stay with me." He would not let her out of his sight. "Let's start in the library."

He opened the door, crept inside, keeping his back to the wall. Vivienne followed, closing the door behind her. Smart woman, he thought. No one could come in or out without alerting them.

Nathan jerked his head toward a couch facing the fire. He doubted the man would be lying on it, but it would keep her out of the way while he checked behind the curtains. The two if them moved silently toward their corners.

Just as Nathan tugged the drapes open, he heard the *swish* of an arrow. He turned just in time to see the assassin raise his knife and hurl it.

At him.

Nathan jerked to the right, and the knife barely clattered against the window inches from where he'd stood.

"You missed!" Nathan yelled.

"So did she," the assassin answered.

Vivienne was already readying another arrow, but the assassin didn't wait. He flung himself at Nathan, and the two men rolled to the floor, Nathan's knife clattering under his desk.

"Nathan!" Vivienne shouted. "I can't get a clear shot."

The assassin's fist collided with his nose, and Nathan head butted him before the man kneed him in the breadbasket. The two tumbled over each other again and again, overturning tables and lamps. He smashed the assassin with an antique bowl and stumbled to his feet. For a moment he thought he'd won, but the man was up again and plowed him in the face.

Nathan saw darkness right before his head hit the floor. Vivienne's scream brought him back and he moved his head right before another fist slammed into it. The assassin pulled the punch but too late. His fist hit the hard wood of the floor.

Nathan grabbed his neck and pushed him off, using his elbow to pop the assassin in the mouth. When the man was down, Nathan hit him again. And again.

He would have punched him a third time, but Vivienne stayed his hand.

"It's done," she panted. "He's unconscious."

Nathan gained his feet, putting his hands on his hips and drawing in gasps of air. It hurt to breathe. It hurt to think. It hurt to exist.

"And my father made me take fencing," he said between breaths. "I told him those lessons were a bloody waste of time."

Vivienne gave him a bewildered look. "What did you want to take?"

"Boxing."

She nodded, drew in a breath. "All of our children will be pugilists."

"Even the girls?"

"Especially the girls."

He opened his arms, and she fell into them. He didn't care if the servants were gathering in the doorway now, if Fletcher was calling for a doctor, if somewhere above a maid screamed.

Vivienne was in his arms. His princess.

His duchess.

# Epilogue

"He's an insufferable *muc*," she said, using the Glennish term for *pig*. The door of the Grecian parlor at the residence of the Duke of Stoke Teversault closed as the Prince Regent made his exit.

"I will not argue." Nathan leaned against one cream and dark lilac wall and watched her pace. His wife's ire was stoked now

She was his wife. *His wife*. After they'd dealt with the business of the dead assassins and the live one, they'd received a letter from Prinny summoning them to an audience at the Duke of Stoke Teversault's ball. Nathan had already planned to attend and to approach the prince, who never missed the annual affair, but he'd thought a formal audience a good sign. He should have listened to Stoke Teversault. The duke had cautioned him against reading anything into Prinny's invitation. Nathan had hoped Stoke Teversault was just being...well, Stoke Teversault. He was naturally sober and restrained. Fortunately, Nathan had the foresight to procure a special license and marry Vivienne before the ball.

Prinny might offer his protection, but she'd have Nathan's in any event.

"Can you believe the way he spoke to me?" she said, striding across the parlor and then back again. Through the open windows behind her, he could see the famous row of lime trees that lined the house's drive. "He acted as though it was my father's fault he and my mother were killed. As though anyone deserves to die that way!"

"He's afraid," Nathan said, moving toward her and laying his hands on her shoulders. "He knows but for luck and the grace of God, that could have been him."

She turned into his arms. "He's allowing me to stay in the country only because of your gift." Her eyes narrowed. "What exactly was this gift?"

"A small token of my fealty." Three ships was a token indeed. "But you are the Duchess of Wyndover now. He couldn't make you leave even if he wanted."

"And so there's to be no outcry over the massacre at Glynaven Palace, no public condemnation."

"Not from England, but you've written dozens of letters to other world leaders. Surely one of them will condemn the actions of the revolutionaries. Perhaps Spain or Russia."

"Perhaps."

He wrapped his arms around her, looked into her lovely eyes. The music from the orchestra Stoke Teversault had hired for the ball swelled and carried on a breeze scented with flowers. "I cannot give you public condemnation. But I can give you revenge."

She stiffened. "What do you mean?"

He touched his forehead to hers. "Happiness."

"Happiness?"

"Did you think I would suggest we hire mercenaries and order the revolutionary leaders slaughtered?"

"It would be a nice gesture."

"You don't want that." Although he imagined a small part of her did, and he could hardly blame her. "Why not be my wife, have children with me, grow old with me? The revolutionaries who tried to kill you, to kill off the royal line, will always know they never succeeded. Our children and our happiness will be the best revenge."

She heaved a sigh of resignation. "You make sense, as usual."

"I am an extremely sensible man."

"You must be to tolerate all those swooning females. Three fainted in your path on the short walk to ballroom."

He scowled, clearly not wanting to speak of the incidents.

"I'm certain the heat overcame the ladies, nothing more. This ball is a crush."

"*I'm* certain it was one look at your pretty face. Oops!" She fell against his chest. "I accidentally looked directly into your eyes.

Help!" She arched back so he was forced to catch her. "I shall faint." Her hand brushed her forehead.

He lifted her off her feet and swept her into his arms. "In that case, perhaps we'd better retire to the bedchamber Stoke Teversault thoughtfully supplied. You'd better lie down, wife."

"Take me to bed, husband."

"With pleasure."

*A Prince in Her Stocking*

## Chapter One

He was being followed. Lucien hadn't seen them, hadn't heard them. Still, he couldn't shake the feeling someone watched him.

Perhaps he was delusional. God knew he came by it honestly, as his mother saw plots and assassins behind every door. The moral of every bedtime story had been not to trust anyone, not to be fooled. The sweet baker wanted to slit his throat, the smiling maid waited for an opportunity to smother him in his sleep.

His father had called it all rubbish, much to his mother's dismay. The king had called it rubbish until the night the *reavlutionnaire* attacked and slaughtered the entire royal family.

In the end, his mother's suspicion hadn't saved her.

It might not save him either, but Lucien couldn't help looking over his shoulder one last time as he stepped inside the bookstore in St. James's. The heat reached out tentative fingers and stroked his frozen face as soon as he entered. He'd quickly learned December in London was colorless, cold, and compassionless. No one had the time or inclination to spare even a second glance at a poor man out in the sleet with only a threadbare coat for protection against the damp and cold.

His face stung as it began to thaw, and he unwound his scarf, exposing his face to the shopgirl, although he suspected she already knew it was he. He came here almost every morning right after the bookstore opened, partly because he wanted out of the cold and partly because he was still searching.

"Good morning, Mr. Glen," the pretty blond shopgirl said in greeting.

It wasn't his name, but when he told people his name was Prince Lucien Charles Louis de Glynaven, they didn't believe him. Mr. Glen seemed easier.

"Good morning, Miss Merriweather. How are you today?"

"Very well, and yourself?"

He was cold and hungry and so tired he could sleep a week. "Just fine. Thank you for asking." He unfastened the top button of his greatcoat, although he didn't intend to remove it. The store was warm, but old books were dusty. He took pains to keep his clothing clean and presentable. He could not afford to soil his coat or shirt, as they were the last vestiges of respectability he had.

"May I help you find anything in particular, Mr. Glen?" Miss Merriweather asked. She already knew the answer. They performed this play nearly every day.

"Just browsing, Miss Merriweather."

The bell above the door tinkled, and a woman of middling years entered On the Shelf, which was the name of the little bookstore in Duke Street. Lucien took the opportunity to slip away, walking along the rows and rows of shelves along three walls of the store until he found the location where he'd left off the day before. The shop was as familiar to him as the lines on his hands by now. It had become an old friend to him, the smell of paper and ink and leather bindings almost as comforting as the smells of the palace in which he'd grown up.

Lucien had no trouble finding the shelf where he'd paused his search the evening before, which was not far from the counter where Miss Merriweather spent most of her time. He took solace in the fact that he was now several shelves deep in his search. He had made progress. Last night he'd ceased searching when he reached the bottom of the shelf, of course. His back had ached by the end of the day, and he'd left the lower shelves for the morning. Unfortunately, he'd spent the last of the money he'd earned tutoring students in Glennish, which meant he'd spent the night in a doorway of an abandoned shop, rather than in his usual spot in a cheap boarding house where men slept twelve to a room on straw pallets infested with lice and other vermin it was too dark to see.

As a consequence, his back felt no better than it had the evening before. He leaned against the shelf behind him and closed his eyes. How much longer could he go on this way? He'd fled the revolution more than seven months before and had been all but living on the streets of London for the last six and searching the bookshop whenever he did not have tutoring work for more than four months. He was hungry, cold, and tired. He didn't want to give up hope, but at some point he must accept that he might never find the goddamn papers. He might never reclaim his title or the money so carefully put away for just this eventuality. He might die on the streets of London, and no one would give a damn.

To the world, he was already dead.

"What is that man doing?" he heard a woman ask Miss Merriweather. "Is he sleeping?"

"Oh, he's harmless enough. I think he comes in to stay out of the cold," Miss Merriweather answered. As he was the only man in the shop—for some reason, the bookshop seemed to always attract more women than men—he assumed the ladies were speaking of him. He wished he had a few coins so he might buy a book today. He tried to do that when he could in order to maintain the illusion of actually patronizing the bookshop.

"Miss Merriweather!" the first lady admonished. "Half of London will be loitering in your shop if you continue to allow this. I must insist you send him on his way."

Lucien drew in a breath and held it. He might be weary of the search, but he was not ready to be forced to abandon it or the little shop he had begun to think of as home.

"Lady Lincoln, I assure you the man is no trouble. Please do not allow him to concern you. Now, just the volume of Fordyce's Sermons today?"

Lady Lincoln sniffed. "Your mother will hear of this. See if she does not."

When the bell tinkled again, signaling her retreat, Lucien

blew out the breath and crouched. He pulled the first volume of a book of poetry from the shelf, opened it, and turned every single page. He liked to think of this as his "no page left unturned" method. He knew it was highly unlikely the papers he sought had found their way into a book of English poetry—mediocre poetry, he decided after scanning a page or so—but all other methods of obtaining the books and documents had failed. He had no other choices, no other options, and so he did the only thing he knew. He searched.

"Will she really tell your mother?" a voice he recognized as the young Miss Hooper, the auburn-haired friend of Miss Merriweather, drifted across the shelves. She'd lowered her voice, but the store was almost empty and quiet, and he knew every sound by now. Lucien paused in his perusal of a poem about a lovelorn shepherd to listen.

"She has nothing else to occupy her time, so I imagine she will."

"Will your mother force him out?" Miss Hooper asked.

"I don't know. Why? Don't tell me you've developed a tendre for him."

Lucien could almost hear the blush rise to Miss Hooper's cheeks. "Of course not, but I do feel sorry for him. Imagine. The poor man thinks he is a prince."

Lucien laid the volume of poetry on the shelf and moved closer. He did not want Miss Hooper's pity—Miss Merriweather's either, unless it served to keep him from being evicted from the shop. Strange to be the object of pity after so many years of being reviled for his privilege.

"I am well aware of his delusions." That was Miss Merriweather's voice. "You forget I was here the morning he stormed in and demanded we hand over the shipment of Glennish books we bought at auction. I had no notion which books or which auction. The man was quite mad with desperation, so I showed him the only books we had on Glynaven."

"But he didn't want them," Miss Hooper said. She knew the story and could have probably told it herself at that point. "And he's come every week since?"

"Yes, and he even apologized for his rude behavior that first day."

"Did he? I am not surprised. He has a very kind look about him."

Miss Merriweather gave a bark of a laugh. "I beg to differ. He has no such thing. He has the look of a gypsy—all that dark hair and golden skin."

"But his eyes," Miss Hooper said with a sigh.

Lucien rolled his oft-mentioned eyes. In Glynaven, poetry worse than the volume he'd just perused had been written about his leonine eyes. They were brown—a golden brown, yes—but brown. He might think it ludicrous, but he was not above using those eyes to persuade the Merriweathers to allow him to continue his frequent browsing. At this point, he was not above anything.

Oh, how the mighty—and haughty—had fallen.

He turned, intent on returning to the shelf of mediocre poetry, and almost rammed into a petite blond woman, who circled her arms frantically for balance. Acting on instinct, he reached out and caught her shoulders, hauling her back to her feet. Lucien realized immediately he wasn't quite as gentle as he might have been. The force of his action sent the woman careening toward him, and he was forced again to right her.

He held her shoulders, ensuring she was finally stable.

"I beg your pardon," he said. "I didn't see you there."

She had the fair complexion typical of the English, and a pink flush crept over her cheeks when he spoke. "It is my fault," she said in a voice little more than a whisper. "Please forgive me."

She wore spectacles, and her eyes behind the lenses appeared quite large and blue. Those were the sort of eyes one should honor with bad poetry. They were the blue of the Mediterranean Sea.

"Excuse me," she whispered, looking down so he had a view of the top of her head of golden hair. She'd pulled it tightly back and secured it at her nape with a black comb.

"If you would release me, sir?"

Lucien released her as though she were poison and stepped away. "I apologize. I didn't realize—"

"No apology necessary. Excuse me." She moved toward a small round table of books in the center of the shop, her black skirts swishing as she moved.

Lucien returned to his shelf of poetry only to find someone

else had taken his place—a woman with a bonnet trimmed in yellow flowers and a black net veil over her hair. He could not see her face. He turned to occupy himself with the novels until such time as the lady moved on, but the shelf of novels was also occupied by a tall well-dressed gentleman and a woman in a dark green redingote. He thought he recognized the woman as the shopgirl from Markham's Print Gallery, which was situated just next door. She often watched the bookshop when Miss Merriweather was away on an errand, and she'd always been kind to him.

The shop was damnably crowded now that the holidays approached. Lucien took a book from a shelf he'd already searched and looked through it in order to appear to be shopping. He wondered about the woman he'd bumped into earlier. She must have been a widow to be dressed in such severe black without any adornment. Was she one of the many women who frequented the shop, or was this her first visit? He did not recall having seen her before, not that he paid much attention to the shop's patrons. He was engrossed in searching the books. He continued his search, ignoring the slight headache from lack of food and drink. Lucien withdrew another book, examined every page, then replaced the volume. Before he withdrew the next, he glanced behind him, hoping he'd see the Englishwoman in black again.

*** 

Cassandra hurried home through the cold, wet streets of London. The day had barely begun, but the sky was as gray as twilight. Worse yet, fog stole in and began to blanket the streets, making everything even grayer and darker.

"Watch your step, my lady," Riggersby, her footman, called over his shoulder. He walked slightly in front of her to lead her through the dense fog. Usually, he walked behind her, but today she needed his help navigating the way back to the town house. "Almost there, my lady." His tone was full of censure, and he had every right to be cross with her.

Riggersby and Vidal, the butler, had both suggested she take the coach to the shops, but she hadn't wanted to go to the trouble. At least that's what she had told them. The truth was, that even after nearly three years as Viscountess Ashbrooke, Cass did not feel comfortable ordering grooms from their warm quarters solely for her pleasure. And she certainly did not want the poor horses out in this foul weather. Riggersby would have taken issue with that opinion—not ostensibly, of course. But she would have read the thoughts on his face: *Not want the poor horses in the foul weather? What of the poor footman?*

She longed to return home and sip a cup of hot tea by the fire. She was almost completely frozen, inside and out. The only part of her that retained any degree of warmth was her shoulders, where *he* had touched her.

A prince had touched her!

Ridiculous notion, she knew. The man was no more a prince than she was a fairy. She'd overheard the shopgirl and her friend speaking of him. Clearly, they did not believe him a prince. Equally clearly, he did believe himself one.

Which made him quite mad. Weren't all the handsome ones mad, though? She'd seen portraits of Byron, and he was quite handsome and, many argued, quite mad.

A man moved aside to allow her to pass and lifted his hat to her. Cass wondered if she knew him, but she could not pause to study him, else she would lose Riggersby. She hurried on, happy to huddle in her pelisse and muff, her head down to keep her face out of the worst of the wind.

Of course the man in the bookshop had not been a prince, though she could certainly picture him in that role. He had all that dark hair and olive skin paired with a face that would have made a sculptor weep. No sculptor would have been able to capture the eyes, though. That color was so terribly unusual and so absolutely breathtaking. She'd seen him in the aisle and moved into it because she wanted a closer look at the "prince," but when he'd caught her and she'd looked into those eyes, she hadn't been able to speak or even breathe.

He must think her an absolute ninny, if he thought of her at all, which she doubted very much. In the meantime, she could still hear his voice, slightly accented when he spoke, and feel his strong hands burn through her dress.

Her ugly dress. Widow's black because her husband had died fourteen months before. She should be ashamed of herself for thinking of another man—*lusting* after another man—as Euphemia, her late husband's sister, would have said. And Cass was ashamed.

Mostly.

"Here we are, my lady," Riggersby said, indicating the steps leading to the front door. He allowed her to climb them first, then rapped for her. The door opened, and Vidal blinked at her with his large owlish eyes.

"You have returned, my lady. Miss Ashbrooke has been worried."

"Oh?" Cass handed Vidal her muff. "Riggersby was with me."

"Is that Cass?" a feminine voice called.

"It is I, Effie. I'm returned and quite well."

Effie moved as quickly as a woman with two canes might, then stopped short when she spotted Cassandra. "Why, you are frozen through! Do come sit by the fire." It was not so much a request as an order, and Cassandra complied because she was quite cold and desperately wanted the fire.

And because she always did whatever Euphemia told her. Cass did what everyone told her. She was meek and malleable and all but mute in company. As a child, it rarely, if ever, occurred to her to object to her parents' dictates, even when they dictated whom she might marry.

That was how she, a merchant's daughter with no title or connections, ended up a viscountess. That was also how she'd found herself married to a man forty years her senior, who had been more like a grandfather than a husband to her.

Euphemia was almost sixty herself now, and when Norman had passed away, she had slid into his place, eager to order Cass about as she saw fit. Although only two years shy of thirty, Cass was not allowed to express a single original idea. No idea was worthwhile unless it was Effie's idea first. Cass had wanted to dress in half-mourning a year after Norman's death. Effie insisted on full mourning indefinitely. Cass had wanted to acquire a cat or a dog, some sort of pet to keep her company. Effie claimed animals were far too dirty to keep inside. Cass had asked the cook to make more-flavorful meals. Effie had objected, saying anything stronger than bland potatoes and boiled beef bothered her stomach.

The few friends Cass had made among the wives of other peers when Norman had taken her out had long since abandoned her. When they came to call, Effie was so unpleasant, they did not return. Cass never went out in Society anymore, and so she saw no one and did nothing of interest.

Some days she wished she had died when Norman had.

But not today. Today she had been touched by a madman who thought he was a prince—that was certainly more exciting than anything else that had happened in the past two years.

Cass followed Effie into the small parlor where they often took tea in the morning. It was not a particularly cheerful room. It had been designed to allow the sunlight to warm and brighten the space, but Effie had decorated it with heavy brocade drapes that were closed unless Cass was in the parlor alone. The furniture was old and worn, upholstered in a faded olive green fabric. Cass would have preferred something lighter and airier, but though she was the lady of the house and should have been allowed to decorate the parlor as she desired, Effie had shown so much resistance to any change in the parlor or the entire house, Cass had not dared.

Now Effie rang for tea and ordered a maid to stoke the fire and bring her a blanket for her lap and a shawl for her shoulders. Very soon, Cass was no longer frozen. Indeed, she was far too warm.

"Girl!" Effie said to the maid. "I am still cold. I told you to stoke the fire."

"Yes, miss."

Effie scoffed. "It is so hard to find good help these days," she said to Cass, who wiped her forehead with her handkerchief. She could not be cross at Effie for being cold. She was so thin and bony, much like her brother had been, whereas Cass was much shorter and rounder. Her hips, touted as perfect for childbearing, had been one of the qualities that recommended her to the viscount, who'd needed an heir. Her hips and her father's money.

Alas, she had not borne him an heir, but her hips were still ample.

"Did you find the thread I wanted?" Effie asked.

"Yes, I did. I found the thread and the fabric. I think you will be able to remake the hat nicely."

"Good." The tea arrived, and Effie prepared it for both of them. Although Cass had said time and again that she preferred it black or with only a dash of milk, Effie made both teas with copious amounts of milk and sugar. Cass found it nearly undrinkable.

"And where else did you go?" Effie asked, eyes narrowed over her teacup.

Cass thought about lying, but Effie would only ask Riggersby, and then she would be found out. "I went to the bookshop."

"Which one?"

"On the Shelf," Cass said quietly.

"Eh? Speak up! None of your mumbling."

"On the Shelf."

"Why ever would you go *there*? It's the haunt of spinsters."

Cass wanted to point out that she *was*, for all intents and purposes, a spinster and so was Effie, but she knew better.

"I wanted a book," she said simply.

"A book?" Effie leaned back and blew out an exasperated breath. "We have books here."

She'd read all the interesting books, and those that remained were dry texts on botany or mapmaking. But what did Effie care, as she never read? That had been the one interest Cass and Norman had shared.

"Well?" Effie demanded.

Cass blinked at her.

Effie sat up in exasperation. "What book did you buy?"

"I…" Cass closed her mouth. "I didn't buy one. I…forgot."

It was the truth. Seeing the prince had made her forget everything, and then she'd been so embarrassed by her clumsiness, she'd just wanted to escape. She couldn't reveal any of that to Effie.

Effie stared at her with a look of disgust. "Well, I suppose my brother didn't marry you for your mind."

## Chapter Two

She was in the bookshop again. She'd come twice in the past ten days, and although they hadn't spoken, he'd seen her come in and known when she departed. Now he looked for her daily. He had a simple life, and it was a small matter to add one more task to his routine—wake, buy a bun or an apple for breakfast if he had the coin, if he had no students he'd go to the bookshop, search the stacks, look for the woman, buy soup or broth if he had coin, find a place to sleep.

These days he did not have enough coin for food and lodging. Most of his students were in the country for the winter. Now that it was cold, he usually chose lodging. He'd always preferred clean, well-tailored clothing, and even as a boy he hadn't liked to be dirty. Of course, he enjoyed playing as any boy might, but he never argued about the bath he had to take as an inevitable result of tromping through mud. Now baths were a luxury he couldn't dream of, but he found he could manage well enough with water, soap, and a clean cloth.

As for food, he was always hungry. Often, he met his students in coffeehouses. Those sessions were torturous because he could smell the delicious stews bubbling in the kitchen but could not partake. Some of his students preferred to meet at their lodgings, and they usually offered refreshment. Lucien was grateful for their generosity. He had not lowered himself to stealing. He was still too proud to join the ranks of common thieves.

The bookshop was crowded this morning. The sleet and freezing temperatures had given the city a brief reprieve, and all of London seemed to want to brave the chilly weather for the chance at feeling the sun on their skin. Lucien had also realized Christmas was near. A smattering of laurel, rosemary, hawthorn, and bay had sprung up outside homes and shops, and he'd overheard people speaking of their plans for the holiday. Of course, families wanted to be together for Christmas. Lucien tried not to think too often about family, and the subject of family Christmases was one forever banned from his mind. If he thought of all he'd lost, he might decide not to go on, and he had no choice but to go on.

Something in the air around him changed, and he looked up from the book whose pages he'd been turning. *She* had stepped near the shelf where he stood and appeared to be studying the volumes at the other end quite intently. She probably had not seen him at this end, and even if she had, she would not remember their first meeting.

He looked back at his book, but as he did so, he thought he saw the flick of her gaze in his direction before she resumed staring at the volumes on the shelf in front of her.

Lucien's heart hammered rapidly. He could not have said why. He was no whelp, inexperienced with women and shy. When he'd been a prince, he'd had to fight the women off. That was not a problem in London, where most probably saw him as little better than a beggar. If women looked at him at all, it was with pity in their eyes.

But Lucien did not think it was pity he'd seen in that brief glance.

He finished the book he was searching, replaced it, and withdrew another. As he did so, he cut his eyes to the petite blond woman again. He did not know her name, but he had heard the shopgirl call her *my lady*. She was obviously a woman of some consequence and, judging from the black crêpe and broad hem of the gowns she wore every time he saw her, a recent widow. He pretended to peruse the first page of the volume he held, but his attention remained on the lady.

She was no great beauty. He had seen great beauties in his life, more than he could count. She was not tall and regal with a slender, willowy form. She was no taller than his youngest sisters, but she was no girl. Her widow's weeds could not hide the lush curves of her body, accented as they were by her small waist.

Her hair was a lovely golden color, though he had never favored blondes. They always looked too pale and lifeless for his taste. Of course, they were not usually blessed with such lovely blue eyes. Those were the widow's best feature, even hidden behind the spectacles. He'd caught a glimpse or two of them, and they reminded him of happier days under warm, sultry skies.

Best not to turn his attention to memories. He could not dwell on the past or all that he'd lost. Instead, he would concentrate on securing his future. He spent the next quarter hour engrossed in his work, though he was constantly aware of her presence just a few feet away. Gradually, she moved along the shelves until she was only two or so arms' lengths away. Lucien knew it was folly to hope that she might wish to become acquainted, but his heart raced nonetheless. How he craved conversation with another, *real* conversation, not pleasant greetings or discussions on verb conjugation.

She didn't look at him again. Her gaze remained steadfastly fixed on the books on the shelf before her. Lucien might have spoken to her, but he did not want the shopgirl ejecting him for disturbing the lady patrons. So he did not speak, though he was excruciatingly aware how long they had been in the same aisle and every single movement she made.

Her hands were small and her gestures graceful. When she read, she tended to cock her head to the left as though pondering the words. And now that they were closer, he thought he'd caught her scent. He knew the smells of the bookstore, of the wood polish and smoke from Mr. Merriweather's pipe, which meant the light, floral scent must be hers.

Unless he imagined the scent, which he did not think an impossibility. It had been so long since he'd been in close quarters with any woman who might have the means to purchase fragrances or bathe frequently, he might have misjudged.

The scent grew stronger, and Lucien had to restrain the urge to inhale deeper. He also forced his head to remain bent, his attention on the history text he held open. He wanted, desperately, to look at her, and because he wanted it so deeply, he would not give in. Everything he'd had, everything he'd wanted, had been taken from him. Desire was dangerous, and he would not give in.

*Thud.*

Lucien's head snapped up when the book hit the floor. For a moment, he thought he'd knocked a book from the shelf.

"Oh dear. Pray, excuse me," the lady said. Her hands were empty. Before she could bend to retrieve it, Lucien had scooped it up. He held it out to her, his eyes touching on the title: *Agriculture in the Roman Empire.*

"It is no trouble."

She took the book, and Lucien wondered if he only imagined that she had dropped the book on purpose.

"You have a lovely accent," she said.

He tightened his mouth to keep it from curving into a smile. He had not been mistaken. She *had* wanted to speak to him. Probably too shy to approach him directly, she'd engineered this meeting. The flush in her cheeks testified to her shyness, but she was not so meek as to allow this opportunity to pass by.

"I might say the same to you," Lucien said.

Her brow furrowed, which had the effect of wrinkling her small nose. "I don't understand."

"Your British accent is lovely." He smiled. "You see, to me, it is you who has the accent."

She stared at him for a little longer than was proper before finally lowering her eyes. "English is not your native language."

"It is not, no." He knew she wanted more, wanted him to answer with detail, but then the conversation might end too soon.

"What is your native language?" she asked.

Oh, he liked her. The boldness of her question made her delicate skin turn from pink to red, but she was brave enough to pose it anyway. He wondered if her nipples were as pale pink as her lips and if they flushed red when she was aroused. The thought was wildly inappropriate and absolutely lecherous, but he was a prince, not a saint.

"Glennish," he finally answered. "Though I speak English, French, Gaelic, and a fair bit of Italian."

"Oh." She looked down at the book she now clutched tightly to her breast. Lucien feared he'd said too much.

Finally, her eyes fastened on his face again through spectacles that were just slightly askew on her nose. "I fear I am terribly ignorant. What is Glennish?"

"It is the language—"

The lad who was often in the shop shelving books and assisting customers passed by, then doubled back after he saw

Lucien and the lady in conversation. As her back was to the lad, the lady did not see him, but Lucien saw and interpreted the lad's glower perfectly. Lucien was allowed to warm himself in the store and peruse the volumes all he liked, but he was not to accost the patrons.

Lucien looked back at the lady before him. As much as he wished to continue to speak with her, he could not risk it. "Excuse me," he said. Placing the volume back on the shelf and noting where he had left off, Lucien made a quick bow and walked away. He strode all the way to the door of the shop and out onto the sunny street.

The weak light warmed him, and the breeze invigorated him. Or perhaps it was the attention from the lady. For a moment, he felt human again, not one of the countless masses populating London.

He would always remember her for that kindness, one she couldn't possibly realize she'd bestowed.

He did have one regret. He did not even know her name.

***

Cass stared at the book in her hand, some dusty volume about Rome, and sighed. What had she done wrong? Why had he left so abruptly? Oh, she was such a ninny to think that a man like him would want to speak to her. He was all tawny skin and broad shoulders, and those sensuous eyes. She'd never used a word like *sensuous* before, but she could not think how else to describe his eyes. When he looked at her, she felt warm all over.

And when he'd smiled…

Lord, she'd thought her legs would fail her. He was the most handsome man she'd ever met, and the first man she had ever wanted so much that she'd dared to approach him. Now she'd had her brief interlude with him, but it was not nearly enough. She wanted more.

She couldn't have more—not because Society forbade it. She was a widow, and Society would look the other way if she chose to take a lover.

The very thought of such wanton behavior made her blush with shame.

But, of course, Effie would not allow such a thing, and Cass did not have the freedom to engage in such a liaison without Effie knowing. Freedom such as that would require her to stand up to Effie, to cause conflict. Cass could think of nothing she disliked more than conflict and discord.

She sighed, feeling despondent despite the pleasant mood she'd been in when she awoke this morning and knew it was another day when she could make an excuse to go to the bookshop. If she went too often, Effie would chastise her. She turned, intending to find a novel to purchase so she would not return home empty-handed, as she had the first time she'd met the mysterious man.

"My lady?" a man said from behind her.

Cass glanced over her shoulder.

"I am sorry to trouble you. I could not help but notice Mr. Glen was speaking to you."

So that was his name. *Mr. Glen.* It was not a particularly foreign name, which made him all the more mysterious.

"Yes," she said, forcing the volume of her voice beyond a whisper. "I dropped a book, and he was kind enough to retrieve it for me."

"I see. I worried he was troubling you."

Now Mr. Glen's abrupt departure made perfect sense. By engaging him in conversation, she'd jeopardized his place here. If he truly came every day, as she'd heard the shopgirl remark, perhaps he had nowhere else to go. And he did appear to be looking through each and every book for…something. He'd left rather than risk being asked to leave for accosting her.

How awful that she'd placed him in that position, when it was she who'd accosted him.

"Thank you for your concern, but he was not troubling me at all," Cass assured him, perhaps a bit too forcefully. "He was very proper and polite," she added.

The clerk nodded slowly, as though he saw right through her to her real motive for speaking with Mr. Glen. "Very well, then. Is there anything I can help you find?"

"Oh yes. I want something exciting. Perhaps *Frankenstein* or *Mandeville*?"

The clerk gave her a wan smile. "Of course."

Walking home, Riggersby behind her with her packages, Cass tried to devise a plan to speak with Mr. Glen again. The only location where she knew she could find him was the bookshop, and yet, if she attempted to converse with him there, she was doomed to failure. He would most likely leave as abruptly as he had today. But what if she could arrange a chance meeting with him outside the bookshop? She had to assume he spent all day inside the bookshop, which meant if she arrived when the shop was closing, he would be leaving. She could ask him to escort her home.

Except she had Riggersby to escort her. Cass looked over her shoulder. She had to find a way to escape Riggersby.

Throughout dinner and Effie's tedious droning on and on about every single ache in her bones, Cass considered. One might have said she schemed, but she had never schemed in her life. She was merely trying to arrange to speak with a friend.

Not that Mr. Glen could be considered a friend... yet.

"Cass, are you listening?" Effie asked, staring at her across the gleaming wood table. Although it was only the two of them, Effie still insisted they dress for dinner and indulge in at least four courses. Effie had very little appetite, so most of the food went back to the kitchens.

Cass did not think the servants minded.

"Of course," she lied. "I was thinking we might ask Allen to make you a tonic. It might relieve some of the discomfort."

Effie nodded approvingly. Her maid was known to use brandy liberally in her tonics, and Effie loved any excuse for her brandy. "That is an excellent suggestion."

Cass smiled. It was so rare that Effie gave her any sort of compliment that she almost felt guilty for not having truly listened to all of the woman's complaints. She would listen diligently tomorrow.

Effie was eager for her tonic and retired early, which meant Cass could also escape to her room. She still resided in the viscountess's room—Effie had not been able to justify taking that for herself—and it adjoined the viscount's room. The master's room was empty now, all of the furnishings draped in Holland covers. It would likely never be occupied again, considering Norman had had no heir, and his will stipulated that in the event there was not an heir, the house was Cass's until she either died or remarried.

Not that she would ever remarry. What man would want to marry her?

Content to wait until Allen had finished with Effie, Cass curled up on the bed and opened *Frankenstein*. She didn't see the words, though. Instead, she tried to remember what it had felt like to have Norman in the bed, lying beside her. She tried to remember a time when she hadn't been alone.

Norman had not visited her bedchamber often, but he'd come often enough that no one could accuse him or her of not having done his duty for the title. But he grew ill only six months into the marriage, and then he was mostly confined to his bed.

She'd spent all day and many nights nursing him, reading to him, talking with him. She hadn't loved him, but she'd had an affection for him. He had been a kind man who had treated her well. She suspected that in his estimation she had been like a loyal dog. One allowed it inside, allowed it to rest by the fire, and fed it scraps from the table. One felt affection for it, patted its head, but when it finally passed away, one went on with one's life and acquired another pet.

She'd slept with Norman, spent his last moments with him, held his hand through the worst of the pain before he'd passed into unconsciousness, but she'd never really known him. They'd both enjoyed reading books, but as to his other passions, he'd never divulged them, nor had he asked about hers. Or perhaps he had, but she had none to speak of.

Now he was gone, and she would sleep in this bed alone for the rest of her life. She'd never know true passion or what it meant to be in love.

The very thought depressed her—and made her all the more determined that her plan to spend an hour with Mr. Glen did not fail.

## Chapter Three

She'd waited for him outside.

Lucien knew what time the bookshop closed, and although he did not have a watch, he knew the closing routine. He did not like to be asked to leave and made certain he was always out of the shop before such a request became necessary.

He trudged out, disheartened that his search had been as fruitless today as every other day, but buoyed by the knowledge that it had not started to rain while he'd been inside. Perhaps he could sleep outside tonight and use the little coin he had to fill his belly.

"Mr. Glen?"

He turned at the tentative voice, half certain he had imagined it. She stood beside the shop window, her bright hair the only relief from the darkness of her widow's weeds.

He covered his surprise with a bow. "Good evening, Miss— Lady—I'm sorry. You have me at a disadvantage."

"My fault entirely," she said with a look over her shoulder. "We have not been formally introduced. I am Lady Ashbrooke."

"A pleasure to make your acquaintance," he said. "I'm afraid the bookshop is closing." He nodded to the door he'd exited. He could hear locks rattling as they were put in place.

"The bookshop?" She seemed to wake from a dream then. If he'd been the arrogant man he once was, he would have attributed her distraction to himself. But here, in his tattered clothing and unkempt hair, he could not fathom why she would speak to him, much less find herself flustered after staring at him.

"Will you walk with me, Mr. Glen?" Another furtive look over her shoulder. Was she looking for someone, or was she fearful someone might be looking for her?

"Of course." He could not allow her to walk about London unprotected. He offered his arm. She took it and all but pulled him away from the bookshop in the opposite direction of the way he'd wanted to go. But of course she was for Mayfair, while he would have ventured west and into the city's rookeries.

"You must think me terribly forward." This was said with her head bowed and her cheeks flushed pink.

"I worry you do not have a footman to chaperone you."

Another look over her shoulder. "Yes. I seem to have lost Riggersby. Perhaps you might escort me home."

"I..." He couldn't refuse to assist a lady in need, but he did not wish to walk all the way into the heart of Mayfair. It would take hours to find a place to sleep, and he did not like walking in the rookeries after dark.

She opened her pelisse and produced a small package wrapped in brown paper. "I just bought these currant buns, but now I find I am not very hungry. Would you like them?"

Lucien's mouth watered at the very thought of currant buns. He'd take her to the ends of the earth for one bite. "I cannot possibly eat your food," he said, his voice strained with the effort it took to refuse.

She looked up at him, her eyes very blue behind her spectacles. "Oh, then I suppose I could give them to a beggar—"

He snatched the package from her hands. "I don't want them to go to waste." Good God, he was only human, after all. He struggled not to rip the paper open as they walked, but he could smell the yeast rising from the package and feel the warmth from the bread. These were freshly baked. His head felt light with anticipation. As they were on Piccadilly now, he did not have the luxury of distraction lest she be jostled or both of them become victims of pickpockets.

"Why don't we stop at Green Park so you might enjoy them while they are still warm?" she suggested.

He liked that suggestion very much, especially as they had almost reached the park. "I wouldn't want your family to worry."

"Oh, I'm not expected home yet."

Interesting. "Won't your family worry when the footman returns home without you?"

She sighed and turned to him. "Mr. Glen, may I make a confession?"

He raised a brow. The woman grew more interesting by the minute. "Of course." He gestured toward Green Park, now visible down the length of Piccadilly. "No one should have to confess all in the melee of Piccadilly. We shall find a park bench."

They strolled along the street until they reached the park, stopping when they found an unoccupied bench. Though it was not raining, the clouds hid the sun, and the park was all but empty. He allowed her to sit and took a standing position beside her to better see the park and any ruffians who might approach.

"Will you sit?" she asked.

"I prefer to stand."

"Will you at least eat the currant buns before they grow cold?"

That he would do. "Would you like one?"

"No. I'm not at all hungry."

He could barely remember what it was like not to be hungry. Lucien struggled to take small, civilized bites of the buns. Still, he finished the first far too quickly. There were three in all, and he vowed to savor the last of the three.

"I suppose I should confess and be done."

Her voice was small and whispery, and he glanced away from the two remaining buns and at her face. It was as red as the falcon on the blue flag of Glynaven. "I promise to be a very lenient priest. The world needs more of them."

"Are you Catholic, then?" she asked.

"Only on the Continent." He rested a foot on the bench and leaned an elbow on his knee. "What is troubling you, my child?"

She smiled at his mock-serious tone. "I'm afraid I did not actually lose my footman."

"I am shocked." He did not even blink.

"I actually sent him on an errand so I might have the chance to meet you." It hardly seemed possible, but her face reddened further, and she looked down at her lap.

"Appalling," he said in a monotone. He had not been wrong in assuming she'd sought him out. Perhaps he did not look as bad as he thought. That illusion lasted only as long as it took him to look down at his scuffed boot.

"It is, isn't it? It's just that I heard Miss Merriweather talking about you, and she said you were a prince. I suppose I was intrigued."

"I can hardly blame you."

She glanced up at him, probably trying to determine if he was in jest. With her face flushed pink and her eyes so large, she looked quite pretty. "You must think me very silly."

"Not at all. Does that mean you believe what Miss Merriweather said?"

"I don't know what to believe."

A breeze blew, ruffling his hair. "Oh, come now, Lady Ashbrooke. That is a very diplomatic reply. What happened to the forward young woman I met earlier?"

"She's gone back into her shell."

That, he could believe. Lady Ashbrooke did not strike him as a woman who took many risks, which made it all the more surprising that she'd approached him. She must be terribly curious. Why not reward her?

Why not satisfy his own curiosity in turn?

"I will tell you the truth about who I am if you promise to return the favor."

Her pretty eyes widened. "You want to know about me?"

"Of course. If I tell you something about me, you must tell me something of yourself. That is only fair, after all."

"I suppose."

"Do not fret, my lady. I will not seek out all your dark secrets." Her lips curled in amusement at that remark. "I will give you leave to ask me three questions, and in turn, you give me the same privilege." This was not a new game to him. He'd played it often at the royal court.

Lady Ashbrooke took her time to consider. The woman was no fool.

"Very well," she finally agreed. "How do we begin?"

He really should have been thinking of where he would sleep tonight. Instead, he rewarded himself with another bite of currant bun. "You ask me a question, and I must answer truthfully."

"But you also have three questions."

He smiled. She was definitely no fool. "Ladies first."

She looked down at her hands again, considering her question. Lucien was disappointed to find his second currant bun gone and even more disappointed to realize he missed seeing her face. When she looked up again, her cheeks were once again pink.

"My first question is, are you really a prince?"

He should have known she would ask that, and he was bound by honor to answer truthfully. "I am. I am Prince Lucien Charles Louis de Glynaven." He gave a little bow, which was more theatrics than courtesy, and was rewarded by her smile.

"Glynaven? I looked it up after you mentioned the language. It's a small country on the Continent. Was there recently a revolution?"

"There was. My father was overthrown as king, and I barely escaped with my life. And that is your second question. My turn."

"What?" She stood abruptly. "I didn't ask a question!"

"You asked if there was a revolution in Glynaven."

"That was a clarification, not a question."

He gave her his best princely stare, but she did not back down. "I'll allow it. This time." He held up a finger. "But from now on, clarifications also count as questions."

"Fine." She sat back on the bench with a huff.

His fingers itched for him to eat the last currant bun, but he wanted to savor it and thus denied himself. Instead of eating, he pondered his first question. Should he ask her if she was a widow? Yes, but how best to ask it?

"Who waits for you at home?"

"I live with my late husband's sister. She will certainly worry if Riggersby returns without me." She twisted a finger of her gloves. "But I am willing to risk the repercussions."

English was not his first language, but that didn't make her statement any less telling. She was a widow, and she didn't like her husband's sister. If the woman frequently imposed *repercussions* on Lady Ashbrooke, he could hardly fault the woman for wanting a brief respite.

Finally, he knew one more fact. She was willing to risk the annoyance, or perhaps even anger, of her family to spend time with him.

He couldn't allow that.

"Lady Ashbrooke, you have no idea how pleased I am to make your acquaintance. It's been weeks since I've had a civilized conversation with another person and months since I have not had to pretend I am only mere Mr. Glen. But there is a reason I choose to eschew my title. You're not safe in my company."

She looked up at him, her eyes wide. "Are you in danger?"

He ran a hand through his hair, which had grown thick and almost to his collar during his months in England. "I don't know. I have every reason to believe I am the last surviving member of the royal family, and I am the heir. If the *reavlutionnaire* realized they didn't kill me, they would stop at nothing to complete the task. I've stayed away from my friends in London, not wanting to endanger them and because I assume that if the *reavlutionnaire* tracked me here, those are the people and residences they will watch."

"But then where are you living?"

He'd scanned the park as he spoke, but now he looked back at her. "That is your last question."

She pressed her lips together. "I know."

"At present, I have no home. I spend my days at the bookshop and my nights wherever I can find a bed."

"Don't you have any funds? Any resources?"

He lifted a hand. "It's my turn to ask questions."

She sighed with obvious frustration. She'd fallen into a very common trap—that of asking all of her questions in rapid succession.

"How long were you married to the viscount?"

"Sixteen months," she answered. "He's been gone over a year now."

He had one question remaining. "You still wear your widow's weeds, though the requisite year has passed. You must have loved him very much."

She looked away, and for a moment he thought he had upset her. But when she looked back, her expression was firm and serious. "The truth, Your Highness?"

He lifted a hand. "Too dangerous to refer to me as such. Mr. Glen will do."

She looked as though she might protest, but then she sighed. "The truth is, Mr. Glen, that I didn't love him at all."

\*\*\*

She'd shocked him by her last statement. How could she have done otherwise? What sort of woman was she to admit she hadn't even loved her own husband? Her *dead* husband. She was supposed to honor him and his memory. She felt like a traitor.

The feeling only intensified when, immediately following her declaration, the prince suggested he walk her home. He'd asked his three questions, and she'd asked hers, and now their acquaintance was at an end. Cass wanted to weep as they entered the quiet streets of Mayfair, and the Ashbrooke town house grew ever nearer.

She'd thought meeting with him would assuage her curiosity and her desire for adventure, but talking with him had only fueled her desire to know more about him. Initially, she'd been motivated by lust. What woman would not have been? The man was dangerously handsome. But the more he'd spoken, the more she'd detected a sadness in him, and a desperation.

The sadness she understood. He'd lost his entire family. What must it be like to be the lone survivor of an entire line? Did he feel guilty that he'd survived when everyone else had perished? She might have asked, if she'd still had questions.

But first she would have asked about the desperation.

She saw the town house just a few yards away and slowed. "We had best part here, Mr. Glen. I do thank you for your escort."

"The pleasure was all mine." He bowed with practiced elegance.

She should walk away now, return home, and make her excuses to Effie. Even the thought made her chest tighten as though a vise had once again been locked into place.

"Will I see you again?" she asked, and then wished she had shut her mouth. How absolutely pathetic she must have sounded. How clinging and desperate.

"That would not be wise," he answered. "Not that I have ever been wise in the past." He tipped his hat. "I will watch until you go inside. Good evening, my lady."

She stared a moment too long and then mumbled her own good-bye. She practically walked on air the remainder of the distance to the town house. What did he mean he had not been wise in the past? Did that mean he wanted to see her again? If there was even a small chance of speaking with him again, walking with him again, she wanted to take it.

Vidal opened the door, and Cass's good mood dissipated. Vidal's expression was severe. "Miss Ashbrooke has taken ill with worry for you."

"Where is she?" Cass handed him her bonnet and gloves.

"In her rooms."

"I'll go immediately." Cass started up the stairs, knowing thoughts of her next meeting with the prince would have to wait.

She gave in to the impulse to see the prince again two days later. Effie was still cross with her for making her worry when Riggersby had returned home without her. Cass had apologized profusely but had not given an explanation for how she and the footman had come to be separated. She did not want to lie, and so, despite Effie's demands and angry outbursts, Cass kept silent. It felt strangely empowering to defy Effie even in that small way.

Riggersby, of course, made no demands, but he had become a hawk. She knew she wouldn't escape his notice so easily again. Cass did the only thing she knew would guarantee seeing the prince again—she went to the bookshop.

She found him one shelf over from where she had seen him last. He was on one of the lower ladder rungs, a volume in one hand. His fingers were blurs as he flipped the pages. He didn't seem to be reading, though his attention was fixed on each and every page. Finally, he closed the book and replaced it on the shelf. She would have needed to be two rungs higher on the ladder to reach that shelf, but he accessed it easily.

As though sensing her gaze on him, he turned her way. His beautiful golden brown eyes warmed but did not seem surprised. At his look, she felt rather warm herself, and she loosened the scarf at her neck.

"Lady Ashbrooke." He nodded. "How good to see you again. Am I in your way?" He spoke formally—as he should, considering they hardly knew each other—but she still had the sense he did so for the benefit of anyone listening.

"Not at all. I saw you browsing and thought I would say hello." Dear Lord. Now she had nothing else to say, and he was still looking at her with those eyes that made her face heat until she thought she might explode. "Uh, hello," she said with a wan smile.

"Hello." His voice was deep and velvet soft, and was it her imagination, or had his gaze dipped to take in her body? It must have been her imagination. Men did not look at her in that way.

She could think of nothing else to say, and when an uncomfortable silence descended, she cleared her throat, hoping he would fill it.

He didn't.

"I should be going."

"Good day to you."

She turned to walk away and simply could not do it. *Stop being a ninny, Cass!* She clenched her hands into fists and turned back. "Unless I can be of some assistance?"

His look was veiled and impossible to read. It was probably some sort of technique all the royals were required to master so they might better negotiate treaties or whatnot. She was behaving in a most abominably forward manner, but he was a man. If he did not want her company, he could tell her easily enough.

She bit her tongue, praying he would not be too unkind.

"I'd like that," he said.

"Of course. I'm so sorry to trouble—"

He was smiling at her. He hadn't dismissed her at all. He'd invited her to help him. Her heart thumped so hard she could not manage to take a breath. Perhaps she hadn't heard him correctly.

"Did you say you would like my help?"

He nodded. "Very much, but I don't want to keep you if you have another engagement."

She shook her head violently. "No. I don't! I have nothing else to do. I'll help you in any way I can. I'll do whatever you ask." Now her cheeks heated for quite another reason.

His gaze seemed to darken, and she feared he would comment on the double meaning of the remark she'd just made. Part of her *hoped* he'd take the double meaning, though she hadn't meant it that way.

Instead, he reached for the next book on the top shelf and handed it to her. He was far too much the gentleman to remark on her ill-advised choice of words.

"It would make my search go faster if you looked through this book."

She longed to ask what he searched for, but this was neither the time nor the place for questions, not to mention she'd used all of hers already.

"What do I do?"

He moved beside her and opened the book. His hand brushed hers as he did so, and she became aware of the warmth of his body and the scent of sandalwood. She swallowed and forced herself to breathe slowly lest she begin to pant.

"I want you to turn every single page and examine it." He spoke softly, his voice low enough that only she could hear. She held the book with both hands now, and his arm slid against hers as he pointed to the open page. "I'm looking for any loose pages or papers slipped inside." He indicated the shelves nearby, most of them filled with unbound books.

"I see." Her voice was but a breathless whisper. "Just the bound books?"

"No. All of them. To be certain." He turned the page, the action bringing his bicep briefly in contact with her breast. Heat surged through her, and she couldn't help but gasp at the shock of sensation. Surely he hadn't even noticed. He had on a coat and she a dress with several layers under it. He couldn't have known he touched her where no man but a husband should.

"If you find anything, show me," he said, withdrawing. He pulled his hand back, and this time he did not touch her. Her face was likely as red as a tomato, and she did not dare to look at him.

"I can do that."

"Thank you."

From the corner of her eye, she saw him take down another volume. She had also noted the kissing bough someone had hung from the ceiling. Evergreens and mistletoe seemed to stare down at her, daring her to kiss the man she desired. Cass swallowed and looked away. At the window, a gentleman who looked every bit the Corinthian stood and pretended to read a novel, while watching the street. The romantic in her liked to think he was watching for the woman he loved. With a sigh and a refusal to spare the kissing bough another glance, she went back to her employment, working beside the prince in silence for at least a quarter of an hour. She turned every single page and scanned it carefully, but her thoughts were not on her task. Her thoughts were on the prince, and they had drifted into forbidden territory.

In her mind the two of them stood in the library of a royal palace. She was dressed as a princess in silks and satins, the likes of which she had worn only during the most choice events of her brief Season. She reached up to remove a book from a bookshelf, and her arms glittered with jewels. She'd barely opened the book when the prince put his arms around her tiny waist. This was only a daydream, so of course she had a tiny waist and such perfect vision that she didn't require her spectacles.

He murmured something seductive in her ear, and she shivered with anticipation. Finally, his mouth lowered to graze her bare shoulder. At the same time, the hand on her waist inched higher to cup her breast. He kneaded it expertly, causing the nipple to harden to an aching point. His mouth continued to worship the skin of her neck, and his other hand slid to the juncture of her thighs.

"Lady Ashbrooke?"

Cass opened her eyes, momentarily disoriented to realize she was not in the palace library but inside On the Shelf.

"Are you well?"

The prince watched her with concern in his narrowed eyes.

"Perfectly. Why?" She realized she'd closed the book and, wanting something to occupy her hands, replaced it on the shelf.

"You were standing quite still with your eyes closed and one hand pressed to your abdomen. Your breathing had grown rather rapid—"

Cass felt her cheeks heat in mortification. "Did you have a library in the palace at Glynaven?"

His brows rose slightly, an indication she'd surprised him with her question. She'd surprised herself.

"Are we playing three questions again, Lady Ashbrooke?"

"Yes." It might not be wise to play the game with him again, but neither had it been wise to approach him today. Besides, she was past the point of acting wisely. She had the rest of her long, lonely life to behave wisely.

He gave her a slow smile, which should have made her question what he would ask her in return. Instead, she rather hoped it would be something scandalous. At that thought, she peered about them. They were the only patrons in On the Shelf at the moment and at the back of the shop, away from the clerks and the doorway. Business was slow today, and Cass heard only the shopgirl humming to herself as she dusted the volumes in the window.

The prince leaned one shoulder against the shelf, tucking the book he held under his arm. "We had a magnificent library."

"What was it like?" she asked, leaning close because he spoke softly so the shopgirl would not hear.

"That's two questions."

She nodded, not caring.

"The chamber was domed, and the cupola was painted by famed Renaissance artists from Glynaven—mythical images of satyrs and wood nymphs and enchanted forests. In the daytime, the library shone with light from the tall windows spaced throughout. If the lawn was not lit with lanterns at night, one could see all the stars from those windows. I used to sit for hours on the red velvet chaise longues and read. Of course, my younger sisters thought it most diverting to sneak up to the second level, squeeze behind a pillar, and spy on me. They must have been exceedingly desperate for entertainment to find watching me read of any interest."

Cass smiled, imagining the girls tiptoeing and giggling as their older brother pretended not to notice them. She'd never had any siblings and had often been so lonely that a chance to spy on an older brother would have been welcomed.

"And now it's my turn," the prince said. "What is your name—your Christian name?"

Cass smothered a smile. He did care about her. He would not have wondered such a question if she didn't hold any interest for him. "My name is Cassandra, but everyone calls me Cass."

He nodded slowly. "Cassandra, the cursed princess of Troy."

Cass ducked her head. "I do not think my parents are great readers. I believe they just liked the name. And I have no great gift of prophecy, though I imagine if I did, no one would believe me either." Fortunately, her head was bowed, and she did not have to look at him when she spoke. She feared she'd revealed too much.

"I have another question," he said quietly, so quietly she had to lean closer to hear his voice. She again caught the scent of sandalwood and took a shaky breath.

"I suppose it's only fair. I asked two in a row." She glanced up at him, saw his lion's gaze on her, and darted her eyes back to the worn boards beneath her feet.

"What were you daydreaming about?"

She froze. The object of the game was honesty, and she could not reveal the subject of her fantasy. She began to shake her head.

"Tell me, Cassandra." The sound of her name on his tongue made her breath catch.

"I cannot," she whispered. "It is too"—*mortifying*—"personal."

"I answered your questions, and remember, you have another yet to ask. You can ask me anything you want, and I'll answer."

His voice was so seductive and so low that it rumbled through her, bringing warm spirals of pleasure with it. She could not tell him what she'd been thinking, and she also knew she didn't have the willpower to deny him anything.

## Chapter Four

He'd pushed her too far. He could see by the way she drew away from him and how she wouldn't meet his eye. He'd asked too much of her too soon, and she wouldn't reveal her daydream. Curse his impatience! And curse his need to know as much about her as he could. There was no point in it. It was not as though he could marry her, or even become her lover. Even speaking with her now was dangerous for her if they were observed.

If the assassins who had murdered his family were in London, and he had to assume they had pursued him, then the best way to protect her was to walk away.

Now.

"I shouldn't tell you this," she said as he found the strength to bid her adieu.

Those words silenced his tongue. It was always the forbidden that made him want more. "But you will."

He moved closer to her because he liked being close to her and because her voice was but a mere whisper.

Her head was lowered, and she wore a black bonnet on her golden crown of hair, but just past the brim he could see her scarlet cheeks.

"I was imaging you and me in a royal library."

Ah, that was why she'd asked about the library at Glynaven Palace.

"Tell me what we were doing in the library, Cassandra." It was a statement, not a question. Even if he'd asked a third question, he did not think she would notice. But he could not risk losing his third question, because he had already decided what it would be.

"You had your arms around me."

He could barely hear her.

"I embraced you."

"From behind, and you'd lowered your mouth to… kiss me. Here." She touched her collarbone, and Lucien had the mad urge to strip away her clothing and kiss that collarbone right then and there.

"This was a fantasy."

Her blue eyes flicked to his face and back down.

"I like it so far. I believe if I had come across a beautiful woman like you in the library, I would have certainly kissed your neck and your shoulder. Tell me what else I did."

"You touched…" She pressed a hand to her abdomen and lifted it so it skimmed over her breast.

His cock hardened at the gesture, and he had to swallow before he could speak again. "There's more."

She shook her head, fiercely this time. "I've said enough. It's my turn to ask a question."

He wanted to know all of her fantasy, but he was not so mad with desire as to think this the time and place. Of course, this was the only time they might have and the bookshop the only place.

"Ask me, then," he said.

The bell above the shop door jangled, and Cassandra jumped. He heard a man's voice greet the shopgirl and then a woman's.

Cassandra cleared her throat and reached for another book on the shelf. He should do the same, pretend to browse lest they be observed conversing.

But he didn't reach for another book. He wanted Cassandra alone, wanted to continue this conversation.

"Come with me." He took the book from her hand, replaced it on the shelf, then grasped her wrist. He knew every exit from the bookshop. He'd found them all the first time he'd come. He always knew every exit from any building where he spent time. Now he pulled her toward a rear door with a bar over it to keep it secured from the inside. At one time the door might have been used for deliveries, but Lucien's investigations had uncovered a back room with a larger door where carts might be more easily divested of their contents. He reached the barred door, glanced about to make certain no one watched, and slipped the bar from its mooring. He'd had to release Cassandra to do so, as the bar was quite heavy and not easily moved after long years of neglect. When the door was open, he indicated she should step out first, and then he followed, closing it behind him.

They stepped into a shadowed lane that ran behind the shops in Duke Street. At one point it might have housed mews, but now they were quite alone. The day was gray and cold, and either the first drops of rain or wet snowflakes dusted his cheeks.

"Why did you bring me here?" she asked, her cheeks still pink from her earlier embarrassment. The color made her look fresh and pretty despite the solemn black of her clothing.

"Is that your question?"

"No, but I think you must know what it is already, else you would not have brought me out here so we wouldn't be overheard."

If that was what she wanted to believe, he would not argue. "You want to know what I'm searching for."

She nodded, leaning her back against the door behind them.

"That is a dangerous question, Cassandra. Suffice it to say I'm searching for proof of my identity, and I have reason to believe it's hidden in one of the books in this shop."

"What reason?"

"That is four questions. It's my turn."

Her gaze met his expectantly, her blue eyes magnified behind the spectacles. Slowly, he lifted his hands and removed them from her face. She blinked at him, her eyes still amazingly large and lovely even without the lenses. He dropped the spectacles into his pocket.

"What are you doing?" she asked. "Without my spectacles, I won't be able to see any distance and make it home."

"Right now, all you need to see is me. Right here. In front of you. May I kiss you, Cassandra?"

She took a sharp breath. "Is that your question?"

He made a sound of acknowledgment, not daring to touch her until she gave her assent.

"Yes," she whispered.

He felt as nervous as a youth kissing a girl for the first time. For a moment, he did not know where to put his hands or how to begin. Then he leaned one hand against the door and placed the other on her cheek. Her skin was cold but soft. His fingers brushed against her silky hair, and his thumb rested on her flesh. Lovely Cassandra, as fair as he was dark. His bronze skin seemed a blot against her pale flesh.

He brushed his thumb over the curve of her cheek, then bent until his lips were a mere fraction from hers. She lifted her chin, anticipating his kiss, angling her head so their noses would not bump. He brushed his lips over hers, his flesh meeting hers with a mere whisper. Still, he felt the jolt zing through him and knew that one brief caress would never be enough. He brushed his lips over hers again, then pulled back enough to see her face. Her eyes were closed and her pink lips parted. He watched as the hand he rested on the door clenched with the effort it took not to crush her against him.

A snowflake landed on his lips, the cold a tonic against the heat generated from the kiss. Lucien could resist her no longer. He fisted his hand in her hair and dragged her body against his, lowering his mouth to hers.

But just as he would sink into the sweetness of her lips, he heard the sound of horses' hooves on the packed dirt of the narrow lane where they stood. He moved instinctively to place his body so he might shield her from view. When the cart finally passed, he handed her the spectacles. "Why don't we walk for a few minutes?"

He would have rather kissed her again, which was why he thought it best to walk. He could not kiss her if he had to focus on putting one foot in front of the other.

She followed him down the lane and then out onto Duke Street, not far from where her footman waited in front of the bookshop. "Riggersby is waiting to see me home," she said, "else I would ask you."

"It probably isn't wise, at any rate." He moved away from the bookshop as he talked, not intending to take her far but wanting some distance from the shop. "I haven't felt watched the past day or so, but I've felt eyes on me before. I believe the *reavlutionnaire* have tracked me here. I'm running out of time."

"Time for what?"

"Time to find the papers I need, the papers that are my only hope of salvation. My mother was not the trusting sort. She was

French, and she watched with horror as the revolution swept through her country. Had she not been married to my father and safe in Glynaven, she knew she would have been one of the first on the guillotine. In fact, almost her entire family was murdered during the first weeks of the revolution."

"I'm so sorry. I've read a little about it. My late husband enjoyed histories, and I read to him after he grew too ill to read for himself. It was a gruesome thing, what happened in France."

She was such an innocent. What could a book show her of the realities of the massacre and bloodshed that accompanied revolution?

"The fate of her family meant she never truly trusted the people of Glynaven. She saw the signs of revolution long before my father. He turned a blind eye to the growing unrest, while she prepared. That preparation might yet save me."

"How?"

It had begun snowing harder now, and those still out shopping were hurrying to finish and retreat indoors. Lucien could hardly blame them. The lack of people made the two of them far too conspicuous. He could see her footman shuffling from foot to foot in front of the bookshop. The man would spot them in a moment.

"Some other time, Cassandra. Meet me—"

Prickles ran up and down his back, as though an unseen hand raked him with sharp nails. He spun around, searching for the source of the danger. That boy huddled in the doorway? That couple with their arms linked? That young clerk pulling his hat down to keep the wet snow off his nose?

He wasn't safe here. He'd endangered Cassandra. "Walk to your footman now," he ordered her. "Don't look back at me. Don't acknowledge me."

"But—"

He gave her a small shove, then doffed his hat as though he'd accidentally bumped into her. "Don't question me. Just go."

Her face paled, and she took a step back, then awkwardly turned and arrowed for her footman. Lucien watched her until the servant noticed her and moved to intercept his mistress, and then he pulled his collar up and walked the other way.

He hadn't walked far before he knew they were following. He didn't know how many, and he didn't know when they'd fallen in behind him, but he knew they were there. Lucien prayed they hadn't seen him with Cassandra Ashbrooke, or if they had, they'd seen nothing more than a man bumping into a woman.

The snow fell more heavily, the heavy clouds hanging low in the sky and turning the afternoon as dark as evening. Lucien had threaded his way toward Piccadilly, knowing the street was busy enough that he might be able to lose his pursuers, but only the poorest or most stalwart were still about in weather that had all the makings of a storm. Lucien pushed against the wind, ignoring the bite of it, until his legs felt weak from the exertion and from hunger.

He chanced a look over his shoulder and wished he had not. He counted three men, too many for him to handle on his own without a weapon of any kind. They had hats and coats, but the quick look he'd managed told him they were most likely Glennish. They had features typical of south Glynaven, where the rebellion had begun and flourished—height, dark hair and dark eyes, and the sun-touched skin so typical of the coast.

He couldn't be certain, but he thought he recognized at least one of the men. If they caught him, they would kill him.

The snow blew more thickly now, and Lucien used it to his advantage. He headed into the wind, even though it depleted his strength. Finally, when he'd gained a small lead, he cut across Piccadilly, darting dangerously close to the few conveyances still on the street. He ran past buildings shuttered tight against the cold and snow, then crossed Piccadilly again, turning down a side street. A broken wheelbarrow sat askew in the middle of the lane, and Lucien crouched behind it. It was barely large enough to hide his broad shoulders, but he slouched down so his head almost touched the dirt and brought his knees up to his chest.

He could only hope the rapidly falling snow would obscure his footprints. Even so, with the limited visibility, if the assassins passed the lane without venturing inside, they would see no sign of him.

Lucien had no way of knowing whether the men had seen him zigzag across Piccadilly and no way to judge the passing of time. He lay for what seemed hours on the cold, hard ground, watching as a light dusting of snow covered his threadbare coat. He shivered, and his empty belly protested its lack of food. The snow-laden clouds had blocked out the dreary winter sun, bringing an early evening. If he closed his eyes now, he would probably be dead by morning.

No one but the refuse collectors would mind, and they might even benefit from the few coins in his pocket and his boots, which had no holes yet. His family was dead, and his people already thought him dead. Only Cassandra Ashbrooke knew who he really was, believed he was the man he claimed to be. Would she mourn him?

Lucien closed his eyes and pictured her face turned up to his, waiting for his kiss. He blew out an annoyed breath and opened his eyes again, forcing himself to sit. He didn't want to die. He wanted to kiss her again, *really* kiss her this time. He wanted to test the weight of her hair with his hands, divest her of those ugly mourning dresses, and hear her laugh.

And he wanted to find those *bluidy* books his mother had sent. All of his searching couldn't be for naught.

Ignoring the ache in his stiff shoulders, Lucien peered around the wheelbarrow. Piccadilly looked all but empty, the passersby merely dark shadows in the gathering gloom of nightfall. Time to find food and shelter for the night.

\*\*\*

Effie had tried to prevent Cass from going out that morning. She'd claimed it was too cold and the snow hid ice that made walking treacherous. But Cass would not be deterred. She wore her warmest dress and pelisse, even though the outer garment was not black.

Lucien had been out in the snow all night. Cass could hardly justify staying warm and safe when he had no option but to freeze.

That was if he'd made it through the night. She'd been terrified when he'd ordered her to walk away from him. She knew he'd been trying to protect her from whoever hunted him. She wished she could protect him too.

She'd thought about it all night and had come to a conclusion.

A conclusion Effie would not like. At all.

Riggersby didn't complain when they stepped outside that morning. The snow still fell, and Cass had to negotiate a few of the larger drifts. Despite her efforts, her feet were wet and cold by the time she reached the bookshop, which had been open two hours by then. It was no little effort to escape Effie. She couldn't ask Riggersby to stand outside with the weather so foul, so she settled him inside and went straight back to the shelf where she and Lucien had been searching the day before.

The shopgirl gave her a knowing smile when she passed by, but Cass just pushed her nose in the air and walked faster.

She turned into the aisle and halted. Lucien wasn't there.

Her heart dived into her belly, and she reached a shaking hand for the nearest shelf. *Lucien.* They'd caught him. They'd killed him. Now she'd never know what it was he sought in these books. She'd never help him claim his true identity.

She'd never kiss him again.

Was it wrong that losing the chance to kiss him again hurt most of all? She was a selfish, selfish creature. For the first time in… well, in her entire life, she'd felt alive. Since she'd met Lucien, she'd risen in the morning with a smile, with hope, with a sense of purpose.

Foolish to believe she might be in love. She did not even know the man, not really. But she respected him, admired him, esteemed him. He was tenacious, kind, an unfailing gentleman.

Or at least he had been.

Were not respect, admiration, and esteem the beginnings of love?

And now her chance had been torn away. She would never know if she could love a man, never know if one might come to love her. She would never know passion. Without him, her life would go on as it had before—long, meaningless days filled with tedious niceties.

"Lady Ashbrooke?"

She turned, and just as quickly as her heart had sunk like a stone, it rose like a bubble. "You are alive!" she gasped, forgetting to lower her voice.

He glanced toward the door and motioned for her to follow him into a shadow farther back in the shop.

"Oh, I see. You've started the next shelf," she said. "That's fast work."

He paused midway down the aisle and faced her. "I have to work fast. I don't know how much time I have left."

"Was it assassins yesterday?" she whispered, because he had been whispering.

"Yes. I lost them in the snow and the crush of Piccadilly, but I might not be so lucky next time. If they track me to the bookshop, I'll have to abandon my search."

"Then we must search quickly," Cass said, pulling down the nearest book and opening the cover.

"No." The prince put his hand on the book and closed it. "There is no *we*, my lady. It's too dangerous for you to be seen with me. I must insist you go home and keep as far away from me as possible."

"You insist?"

"Yes. This is good-bye." Like the royalty he was, he took her gloved hand, bent, and brushed his lips over the back. Then he stepped away and nodded a dismissal.

Cass didn't move. She wanted to move. Everything in her urged her to move. She'd always done as she'd been told. She never argued or disobeyed or remotely considered the idea of defiance. But her chin had risen stubbornly, seemingly of its own accord, and her hands had landed on her hips.

"I don't think so." She shook her head. "No. This is not good-bye."

The prince's golden eyes narrowed, much like an angry lion's. "I say it is, and I bid you *adieu*." He moved away from her.

"I don't accept." Cass raised her voice, causing him to retrace his steps.

"Shh!"

"I am not one of your subjects, Your Highness. I am a subject of King George, and as such, you have no authority over me. You need help, and I'm not abandoning you in your hour of need."

The prince gave a rather undignified bark of laughter. "Well said, but I'm afraid you are more of a distraction than a help." He leaned close, so close his breath caressed her cheek. "When you are near, I can't seem to stop imagining kissing you."

Cass was momentarily speechless. No man had ever said such a thing to her. She was relatively certain no man had ever thought such a thing about her. Oh, she was most definitely not leaving now.

"Be that as it may," she stammered, wishing with her whole heart that she did not blush so easily, "I can help you, and not simply by looking through books."

He raised a brow.

"Now, hear me out," she began.

"Never a good beginning."

He was probably correct, but it was too late to go back now. "The men who are after you don't know you and I are... friends. I propose you stay at my town house until the threat has passed."

He huffed out a breath, but she ignored him.

"You have nowhere else to go—I know you don't, so do not pretend otherwise—and the weather is not fit for man or beast. If the snow continues like this, half the city will be under a foot of white. We have beds, coal, and plenty of food and drink. I couldn't forgive myself if I didn't offer you the most basic of English hospitality."

More to the point, she couldn't forgive herself if she allowed him to walk out of her life without a fight.

"What you suggest is impossible," he said, the words spilling out as soon as she'd taken a breath. "My presence alone would endanger you, your servants, and your friends. I will not put you in jeopardy."

The words had barely escaped his lips when the sound of crashing glass made them both cringe and drop to the floor. The prince pulled Cass under him, using his body to protect her as more glass shattered.

# Chapter Five

They'd found him. He didn't have to assess the situation, or even see the shattered glass, to know this was the moment he'd feared. And his worst fear—that he had put Cassandra Ashbrooke in danger—was also realized. She lay under him, her small body trembling with fear.

Around them, the sounds of chaos erupted—a woman screamed, a man cursed, and something crashed to the ground—but in this back area of the bookshop, it was only him sheltering her, her warm body under his, her sweet feminine scent making him long to bury his nose in her hair.

"My lady!" Booted footsteps neared, and Lucien reluctantly sat on his haunches. The footman he recognized as the one always with Cassandra appeared before them. He spotted his mistress lying on the floor, and his ruddy face went pale. "Lady Ashbrooke! Are you hurt?"

Cassandra sat up and lifted a hand to her collar, a gesture that made Lucien smile. His mother always lectured his sisters when they appeared rumpled or disheveled before her. *A true lady is always straight and neat.*

Lucien had thought true ladies must never have much fun if they always had to worry about mussing their hair or muddying their dresses. He rather liked a rumpled lady, but being older now, he could also appreciate more refinement and elegance. Cassandra Ashbrooke had both in abundance.

"I'm quite well, Riggersby," Cassandra told her man. She struggled to her feet, her legs tangled in her skirts, and Lucien offered a hand. The footman gave him a dark look and shouldered himself between the two.

"A ruffian has thrown rocks through the shop window," Riggersby told his mistress. "I must see you home immediately."

But Cassandra was having none of that. "Is anyone hurt? Has the Watch been summoned?"

Riggersby gaped at her. "I couldn't say, my lady. I only know I must see you safely home."

"I'll hardly tuck tail and run if someone needs me," she said, and pushed past him toward the front of the shop. Lucien followed, but the footman blocked his path.

"And just where the devil do you think you're going?"

Lucien nodded toward where Cassandra had just disappeared. "To see if Lady Ashbrooke needs any assistance."

"She's my responsibility. You can go to the devil."

Lucien had had enough of pesky interlopers—be they footmen or assassins—bullying him. He shoved the man against a shelf and glared down at him. "She is my responsibility too, and you'd best take care not to stand in my way."

He shoved away from the servant and stalked after Cassandra. He hadn't anticipated speaking the words he had, but neither did he wish to retract them. She was his responsibility, whether he wanted the duty or not.

Cassandra stood beside the shopgirl, who was crying, and seemed on the verge of hysterics. Cassandra patted her shoulder, and both women stared at the wreckage that had once been the window. As the footman had said, two large rocks sat on the floor, having been thrown through the glass. The cold air and snow had already begun to penetrate.

"I d-don't understand," the shopgirl sobbed. "Who would do such a thing? And to think we almost lost that window, but Lord Wrathell caught the lady. And now it's broken!"

Cassandra glanced at him, and he gave her a slight nod. He couldn't know for certain, but if it hadn't been the Glennish assassins, he would have been very surprised.

"What can we do for you, Miss Merriweather?" Lucien asked. "Shall we send Lady Ashbrooke's footman to fetch your parents?"

The muffled sound behind him attested to the servant's displeasure at the suggestion.

"Oh, would you?" The pretty shopgirl looked from Cassandra to Lucien with teary eyes. "Charlie tore out of here after the rogues."

"Of course." Cassandra turned back to her man. "Miss Merriweather will give you the directions. Go and fetch her parents directly."

"But, my lady, I must see you home."

"I'll do that," Lucien volunteered.

"But—"

"Riggersby!" Cassandra seemed to have found her voice. Lucien liked a woman who stood strong in a crisis. "Do not argue. If Miss Ashbrooke takes you to task later, I will claim full responsibility."

Riggersby glowered at Lucien. "Yes, my lady."

While Miss Merriweather instructed Riggersby, Lucien took Cassandra's arm. "I think it would be better if we leave now, before they have a chance to come back."

She looked up at him, her eyes even wider than usual behind her spectacles. "Do you think they will?"

"No, but I don't like to tarry."

They took their leave and stepped out into the cold. The bitter wind and snow weren't quite as much of a shock as they might have been, considering how quickly the temperature in the bookshop had dropped after the window was broken. Still, Lucien shoved one hand in his pocket, his other being free and icy so that

Lady Ashbrooke might hold his arm. Like the other people out and about, they walked quickly with their heads down.

"When we reach the house, you will come in and warm yourself," Cassandra said.

Lucien made a sound of protest.

"You will," she argued. "I cannot possibly send any man out in this weather, and if there is danger, I am most certainly already in it."

Lucien did not mention that she'd sent her footman out in the snow, but he could not argue her other point. If the assassins had tracked him to the bookshop, they might very well have seen him with Lady Ashbrooke. And that meant she wasn't safe, even in his absence. Was it merely the desire to be warm and fed that convinced him she was actually safer with him present? If the assassins did attack her home, he could defend her. He was already on guard for any possible attack. Would her household staff be so alert?

"Very well."

She glanced up at him quickly. "Then you will come inside?"

"I will."

"And you will stay?"

She didn't add *the night*, but it was implied. "I will. I'll protect you until I can make a plan to leave London, and when I go, I'll lure the assassins with me." He would never find what he sought now. He would have to give up his hope of any sort of future beyond merely eking by. But Cassandra was worth the sacrifice. She was worth that and much more.

"Is that wise? Leaving London? What about the bookshop and the papers you seek?"

"There's nothing for it," he said, not allowing the despair to sink in. There would be time to wallow in self-pity later. "If I want to stay alive, I must flee." Run like a coward in the night. Good God, but he hated himself sometimes.

She looked as though she might say more, but the wind kicked up just then, and they both had to focus their attention on making their way to Mayfair. Lucien tried to look behind him, tried to make certain they were not followed, but it was an impossible task. The snow fell too quickly.

Finally, they arrived. The door to the town house was opened by a very English-looking butler. "My lady, Miss Ashbrooke was worried." The butler spoke to Cassandra, but his gaze was locked firmly on Lucien.

Behind the servant, a curved staircase led to the upper floors. The banister was swathed with Christmas greenery. Shiny red apples and hellebore added splashes of color. The scent was sweet and fresh as a meadow.

"I'll speak to her directly, Vidal." Cassandra gestured to Lucien. "This is my friend…" Here she paused and seemed to consider how to introduce him.

"Mr. Glen," he said, bowing. "Lucien Glen."

The butler looked down his nose at him. "I see. And where is Riggersby?"

"There was an incident at the bookshop," Cassandra explained, unfastening her pelisse and handing it to Vidal. "I sent Riggersby to fetch Mr. and Mrs. Merriweather as Miss Merriweather was there alone."

"What sort of incident?" a shrill voice interrupted.

Lucien's attention snapped to the top of the stairs, where a thin woman with a rather yellow pallor stood, clutching her throat.

"Some ruffians threw a stone and broke the shop window," Cassandra explained, sounding very calm and composed. One might never have guessed that she'd been trembling beneath him when the glass had shattered.

"Oh, dear me!" The woman, clutching the stair rail, took several steps toward them. "You are not to return there. You must stay home."

"I will not set foot outside again today, Effie," Cassandra told her. "And I've invited Mr. Glen to stay with us as well."

"What?" That exclamation came in unison from the Effie woman and the butler.

Cassandra seemed unconcerned by their astonishment. "Mr. Glen is a friend, and he is in need of shelter for a few days. I've offered my home."

"A *few days*!" Effie sputtered. Lucien could only assume the butler was too shocked to speak. "You cannot allow a man to stay here for an hour, much less a few days."

"Perhaps I should wait in the parlor," Lucien said.

"That's not necessary." Cass placed a hand on his arm. "I have offered my home, Effie, and I will not change my mind now. There's nothing scandalous in it. You are here to chaperone, and it is not as though I am an unmarried miss. I am a widow."

"Exactly!" Effie pointed a bony finger at her, and Lucien could have sworn Cassandra shrank back slightly. "You dishonor my brother's memory, bringing your lover here!"

"My lover? He is not my lover, and even if he were, this is *my* house. It was left to me by Norman. I may have any guest here I choose, and you can be certain that were Norman still alive, he would certainly offer the same hospitality I do to a friend in need."

"How can you—"

Cassandra held up a hand. "That is all I shall say on the matter. It is decided. Vidal, have the maids prepare a room for Mr. Glen, and then inform Cook we will have three for dinner. Tell her I want her to serve the best she has. No bland dishes tonight. I want wine and flavor and dessert."

Lucien's belly rumbled at the thought. The butler, obviously reminded of who his true employer was, scurried away to do the viscountess's bidding.

"Well!" Effie huffed. "If that is the way it is, then you will have to do without me. I shall not eat at your table. In fact, as soon as the snow has passed, I will remove myself from *your* house."

Cassandra sighed, as though she'd expected this response. "There's no call for that, Effie. I promised Norman I would take care of you, and there will always be a place for you here."

"My dear brother would be shocked were he here now."

"He is not here now," Cassandra said. "He has been dead for over a year."

Effie gasped.

"My period of mourning is over." As if to illustrate that point, she ripped off the black bonnet she wore. "I will never disrespect Norman's memory, but neither will I hide in my room, waiting for my time to die. If you choose to leave, that is your decision. If you choose to stay, know this: There will be changes."

Effie all but fled in horror, and Lucien clapped quietly. "Brava! That was well done. What do you do for an encore?"

She gave him a shaky smile, and he realized just how much the confrontation had cost her. "Cassandra, do sit." He steered her toward a small, stiff-backed chair against a wall. "Why are you shaking? You were brilliant."

"I feel as though I will be sick." She tried to lower her head into her lap, but he caught her chin.

"No, you won't. I don't know your late husband's sister, but I venture to guess that dressing down was well deserved and well past due."

"I should not have spoken to her thus!" she protested.

"You're right." He crouched beside her. "You should have told her off with much more colorful language."

Cassandra laughed lightly. "That is not what I meant, and you know it."

"No. What I know is that you are beautiful and strong and brave."

She gave him a look of incomprehension. "I'm none of those things."

"You are all of them and more."

Behind them, the butler cleared his throat. "Mr. Glen, if you would follow me, I will show you to your room."

"Thank you," Lucien said without taking his eyes from her.

"Will you tell me what you were looking for in the bookshop?" she asked, her voice so low only he could hear. "Over dinner? Will you finally tell me?"

He nodded. "I'll tell you every detail."

*** 

Several hours later, he had bathed, slept, eaten a small meal of bread and cheese, and dressed in clean clothing, which he suspected had belonged to the late Viscount Ashbrooke. They smelled of tobacco and mothballs. They were a bit small for him—the viscount had been shorter and thinner—but they were clean, and if he did not move his arms too much, the tight coat would not bother him.

When the butler summoned him to dinner, Lucien followed the man to the dining room, where he found Cassandra already waiting. "My apologies." He bowed. "I have kept you waiting."

When she didn't speak, he looked up. She stared at him as though he were a stranger. He looked down and immediately realized she must be shocked to see him in her dead husband's clothing.

"I do apologize. I found the clothes laid out after my bath. Should I change back?"

"No! It's not the clothes. I mean, it is strange to see you in his clothing, but that is not it." Her words bubbled up, sounding as though she'd had to force them through a tight throat.

"Then what is wrong?"

"Nothing. It's only… you are so impossibly handsome."

He felt the slow smile on his lips.

"I am certain you must have heard that a thousand times, and I suppose I did know you were handsome." Her cheeks were flaming red now. "But seeing you dressed properly, with your hair washed and your stubble shaved, it's rather a shock."

"A pleasant shock, I hope." He stepped closer, far more pleased by her compliment than he ought to have been. Of course he'd heard such flattery a thousand times—she was correct—but he had never thought of it as much more than flattery. He could see in Cassandra's eyes that she meant it, and he could also see the effect on her. She was doubting herself now.

"I—Lord, I have behaved like an idiot. If you will excuse me."

"I will not." He took her hand before she could escape. "You can't possibly be thinking of forcing me to endure Miss Ashbrooke's company alone."

Her hand trembled in his. She wasn't wearing gloves, and her skin was very soft and very pale. "Effie has chosen to dine in her room."

"Good. Then we shall have the evening to ourselves."

"But—"

"Cassandra, I want to dine with you. You really do not see yourself, do you?"

"Of course I do."

"Then you don't see what I see." He drew her closer and would have taken her into his arms if he hadn't known the footmen were on the other side of the door, waiting for them to take their seats so they might serve the first course. "I look at you and see a beautiful woman. That rose-colored gown is the perfect shade for your skin, the neckline just modest enough but teasing me with a hint of what lies beneath."

It did not seem possible, but her cheeks reddened further.

"And I don't think I've told you how much I love the color of your hair. It's like spun silk. And your eyes—"

"They're behind spectacles!"

"That takes nothing away from their blueness or your beauty. You cannot possibly think of denying me the sight of you at dinner tonight. If you do, you will also force me to break my promise."

"What promise?"

"I vowed to tell you my story."

"Oh." She looked at the table then, and he knew she would stay. Her interest in his tale was much more incentive than any compliment he might give her. He would have to remember that.

He moved his plate to the seat close to hers, so they would not be at opposite ends of the table, then she rang the bell and the first course arrived. Lucien could not speak for the first three courses. He was so completely focused on the food. It was not until the fourth course was set on the table that he'd eaten enough to realize he'd been utterly silent for the past three-quarters of an hour.

But when he looked at Cassandra, she was smiling at him.

"I have been an intolerable bore," he said. "Forgive me."

"There is nothing to forgive. I knew you were hungry that day I brought you currant buns. You must have extraordinary willpower to have eaten them so slowly."

"One does try to remain civilized."

"Oh, some days I do wish we could send civility to the devil."

"And what would you do? If we sent civility to the devil?"

A flush crept up her cheeks.

He grinned. "Ah, we shall come back to that later. First, I believe I owe you a tale. I must earn my keep."

"You do not need to sing for your supper."

"I would have told you even if you hadn't fed me. As I told you before, my mother was a suspicious woman. She had been born in France, and though the people of Glynaven loved her—or at least they seemed to—she never saw them as fully *her* people. Not the way my father, the king, did." He paused as the fourth course was taken away and the fifth presented.

"Perhaps that was why she heard the first strains of discord before any of the rest of us. She saw the unrest brewing and knew the inevitable result. My father shook his head at what he called her silly ideas, and my siblings and I followed his lead. I suppose I knew more of the situation than the other children, being that I am the eldest and the heir. I knew about the accusations the Parliament made against my father. They claimed he stole money from the treasury and imprisoned innocents with secret letters."

"Was any of that true?" she asked, bringing him back from the stone chambers of Glynaven Palace and into the cozy dining room in London.

"I suppose every accusation has a kernel of truth at the center. My parents were the king and queen. They lived lavishly, and they had enemies. But my father was not a cruel man or an unjust one. I believe he would have listened to the dissent if the leaders had come to him. Instead, they chose to attack his private guard. Such an attack angered my father, and he instituted curfews and curbed other privileges that sent many to prison for seemingly small infractions."

Cassandra poured him more wine, and he realized he'd drunk all of his and his throat still felt dry. "My mother warned him of the dangers, but he didn't listen. He saw the uprising as a trifle stirred up by a few malcontents. I don't think any of us, save the queen, realized how persuasive the *reavlutionnaire* were and how easily convinced the people were to follow their cause.

"One night, not long before the massacre, my mother called me to her private chamber. She showed me a stack of old books. Most were Glennish, but a few were English and French. As I watched, she opened one of the volumes and ripped out several pages. Then she secured an envelope with money and papers inside. One of the papers had the name of a bank and an account number. In that account, she had secreted hundreds of thousands of English pounds so that, in the event of an uprising, the royal family could flee to London and live there until peace could be restored in Glynaven."

"So that is why you look through all the books. She didn't tell you where she was sending it?"

"Her most trusted adviser took custody of the shipment of books, and he set sail for England only a day or so before the palace fell. My mother thought it wise to hide the money and papers in a book, because though the adviser might be searched and his personal artifacts rifled, she did not think the sailors would take much interest in a pile of old books."

Cassandra leaned forward. "She is an amazingly intelligent woman."

He nodded and sipped his wine again. "She was. She died in the massacre. All of them did."

Her hand was warm when it covered his. "I'm sorry. I'm certain you must miss them, especially at Christmas."

She did not know the truth of her statement. While some in London festooned shops and wished everyone happy now that Christmas was nearing, most Londoners took little notice of the upcoming holiday. In Glynaven, Christmas had always been the biggest celebration of the year with a week of merriment preceding it. He and his family decorated, sang songs, put on plays, and made each other gifts. The family also followed the German tradition of a Christmas tree.

Lucien glanced at the bowl of cloved oranges that stood in the center of the table. "I do miss them, but your greenery reminds me of happier times."

She tightened her hand on his. "Effie tells me it is bad luck to bring the evergreens, holly, and ivy inside before Christmas Eve, but I like to enjoy it. We'll have a Yule log and an extravagant dinner on Christmas. The servants will play snapdragon and sing carols at the top of their voices. You must stay and celebrate with us. It's only two days away."

"Thank you." She was unfailingly welcoming and kind. He did not know if he would still be in London, still be alive in two days, but at least he did not face the prospect of a cold Christmas alone.

She tried to release his hand, but he held firm. She couldn't eat with only one hand, but he suspected she was no longer hungry for food. He was not. He wanted her touch.

She took a breath. "How did you escape the massacre?"

"I was not in the palace when the *reavlutionnaire* attacked. I had been out with friends and heard the palace was sacked. I rushed to the palace, but it was too late. The grounds outside swarmed with bloodthirsty men and women. I was recognized instantly and chased through the streets of the capital. I finally made for the quay and swam to a British ship anchored in the harbor. The sailors pulled me on board and set sail at the next tide for home. They feared the violence in the city might spill over, and the captain was wise to sail immediately. I later heard many of the ships who tarried were burned or plundered when the *reavlutionnaire* tired of looting the palace and the city."

Her hand gripped his again. He glanced down at it, but her attention was riveted on his face. She must have forgotten he'd claimed her hand.

"What happened to the adviser?" she asked. "Did he sell the books to On the Shelf?"

"No. I found his rented flat, but he was no longer there. The current occupants sent me away, claiming they had never heard of the man. I hired an investigator. I did not know how precious the few coins I had with me then would be. I squandered them and hired the best, who found out that Absolon was murdered in a housebreaking."

"You don't believe that."

He smiled without humor. She did not miss anything. "No. I knew the assassins had found him and staged the murder to look like a theft. They'd probably been looking for valuables, but they did not know where to look or even if he had any with him. They took personal items, like his pocket watch and the silver candlesticks, but the books were untouched."

"Lucien." The word was a breath on her lips.

He stilled, then lifted her hand to his mouth. "Say that again."

"Say what?" Her cheeks were pink.

"My name. I believe that is the first time you have said my name."

She ducked her head. "Lucien."

He wanted to kiss her, wanted so desperately to pull her close. Instead, he would finish his story. There was not much left now. "The investigator told me the books and all of Absolon's belongings were sold to pay the rent still owed. I used the last of my meager resources to pay the investigator to track down the buyer of the box of Glennish books. There had been an auction, and the auctioneer had clearly noted the books went to The Duke Street Bookshop. From there it was an easy task to go to Duke Street and find the shop. The name of the shop had been painted over, but it was full of books. The Merriweathers tell me they have no record of buying any books from the auction, but they must have. Else, where would the books have gone?"

She lifted her wine and drank. "But why would they lie to you?"

"I do not know. People lie. They kill. They loot and pillage. Perhaps it is human nature."

"Perhaps, but suppose I go back with you tomorrow and we speak to the Merriweathers together? They might give us more information if I am with you and inquire."

Lucien had little hope that any more information would be forthcoming, but as a viscountess and a patron of their shop, the proprietors would be anxious to please her.

"You would do that for me?"

"Of course." She lifted her free hand to her pink cheek. "Shall we retire to the drawing room? Or would you rather be left alone to your port and cigars?" She smiled, and dimples appeared in her cheeks.

"I'd rather stay with you," he said honestly.

She led him to the drawing room, which did not look to have been refurbished in the last fifty years. The upholstery reminded him of that favored by his grandmother in her chambers. Everything was of good quality and very well maintained, but he knew instantly the style was not Cassandra's. She would not have chosen the dark burgundy velvet drapes or the dour gold paper-hangings on the walls. He had not seen her private chambers, but he suspected they were light and airy and cheerful.

He sat on one couch, and she took the one opposite, both of them with a glass of untouched wine in their hands. Lucien looked up at the portrait of the old man above the fireplace. He could imagine that man wearing the clothing he now wore. "Your husband?" he asked, nodding to the painting.

"Yes. That was painted a few years before we married."

He studied her face as she looked at the portrait. There was no trace of sadness in her eyes, no softness either.

"And you never loved him?" Lucien asked, perfectly aware the question was impertinent whether he was in England or Glynaven.

She cut her gaze to him. "Not in the way you mean. He was like a father."

"Or a grandfather, I imagine."

She glanced down. "It was a good match. My parents are wealthy merchants, and this was their plan to gain a title. Unfortunately, I never conceived, so the line ended with Viscount Ashbrooke. I fear I've been quite a disappointment to everyone."

"You?" Lucien rose and took the place beside her. She moved over to make room for him, though he had purposely sat close. "Did he even come to your bed?"

She made a sound of shock, but he did not believe she felt it. "I cannot possibly answer that question."

"Why? Don't play that I've shocked you, else I'll believe you are still an innocent."

"He came to my bed," she whispered, staring determinedly at her small white hands, clutched in her lap.

"And was there passion?"

"There was duty."

"I see." He moved closer to her, heard her inhale sharply. "Have you ever wondered what it might be like if there was passion?"

She swallowed, her gaze never rising to meet his. "Yes."

"Would you allow me to show you?"

Now she looked up at him sharply. In the candlelight, her eyes were luminous and so dark blue. "You are a prince. Why would you want me?"

"What man would not want you? I want you, unequivocally. The question, Cassandra, is, do you want me?"

# Chapter Six

Was the man daft? Of course she wanted him. She was in love with him. Initially, she'd fallen in love with his golden eyes, his handsome face, his thick, dark hair. But now she saw the man inside the godlike trappings, and she loved that man.

"Would you think me a lascivious wanton if I said yes?"

His mouth curved in a suppressed grin. "No. I would think myself the luckiest man in the world. Shall I come to your room when the servants are abed?"

She shook her head. Her room was too near Effie's. "I will come to yours."

He reached up and stroked her cheek. She had the urge to lean into his touch, like a kitten craving attention. "If you change your mind and do not come to me, I will understand."

Oh, foolish man. To think she would change her mind. "I won't."

He withdrew his hand, but she could still feel the heat of his touch.

And now she was eager to go to her chambers. The sooner she retired, the sooner he would touch her again—touch her all over.

She made a show of yawning. "Mr. Glen, I find myself suddenly quite weary. Will you forgive me if I retire early?"

"There is nothing to forgive. I will retire as well." He winked at her, and she summoned the footman to light them to their chambers. Allen helped her undress and prepare for bed. When Cass dismissed the lady's maid for the night, she dug into her wardrobe until she found a pretty nightgown her mother had bought as part of her wedding trousseau. She'd never worn it, fearing the small pink bows and light filmy material made her look too young. Now she slipped off her plain woolen nightgown and donned the much thinner one. She covered it with a robe, lest she freeze, and sat by the fire, brushing her hair. It gave her hands something to do while she waited for the house to quiet. Finally, when the bracket clock on her bedside table read midnight, she blew out her candles and crept into the hallway.

Lucien's room was on the other side of the town house, and she had to pass Effie's room to reach it. She tiptoed, her feet bare and freezing, avoiding the boards that creaked. She half expected Effie would throw open her door and scream, "Harlot!" at her, but her door remained firmly closed.

Finally, Cass stood outside Lucien's room. She wondered if he'd fallen asleep and if she should knock or simply go inside. She lifted her hand, but the door opened before she could rap.

Lucien stood in the opening, his shirt untucked and open about his throat. His hair was mussed and his feet bare. He took her arm and pulled her inside his room, closing the door and locking it once she was inside. Now that they stood facing each other, she found it impossible to look away from him. His skin was burnished gold in the low firelight, his eyes like a predator's on the hunt.

But she did not feel hunted. His appreciative gaze swept over her, and she felt like the most beautiful princess in the world.

"You came," he said simply.

"I couldn't stay away." Her voice sounded strange, low and throaty.

"May I kiss you?"

He was such a gentleman. She loved that about him, but she would never survive this first time if he insisted on gaining her approval at every turn. "Are you always so polite when you take a woman to your bed?"

"There is no correct answer for that dangerous inquiry," he said, raising a brow. "But I would never force myself on a woman."

"I am here of my own volition." She stepped toward him, winding her arms around his shoulders, moving quickly before she could think too much about what she did. "I want what you want."

She kissed him. She'd never been so bold, but then again, she had never wanted a man in the way she wanted Lucien. Her lips touched his, and she felt as though her entire body lit with heat and desire. His mouth moved tentatively over hers at first, matching her slow and deliberate explorations, but soon he kissed her deeper. His hands fisted in her hair, and he took her mouth with a ferocity that made her breath catch.

Her body throbbed with need when his tongue delved inside her lips, stroking her tongue and teasing her gently, then more insistently. He possessed her, until all she knew was Lucien. Her hands were on him, under his shirt, fingers trailing the hard muscles of his back and the flat planes of his abdomen. His hands must have touched her too, because she felt the cool air on her arms when he slid her robe off her shoulders.

He made a strangled sound, and she opened her eyes.

He said something in a language she did not understand, and then he repeated, "Where the devil did you get that?"

"It was part of my trousseau, and I've never worn it. Is it too scandalous? Shall I take it off?"

"Oh, I want you to take it off." He lifted a hand to run the backs of his knuckles over the slope of her breast, almost visible under the transparent material. "But not yet."

He kissed her then. He kissed her lips, her jaw, her shoulder, her breasts. He lifted her and carried her to the bed, then began again, kissing every single inch of her.

She thought she would blush with mortification when his mouth found her slick core, but she enjoyed what he did far too much to feel embarrassed. She was naked beneath him, flushed with pleasure, when he pulled his shirt over his head and tossed it on the floor.

She caught her breath. Lucien had his hands on the fall of his trousers, but he paused. "Shall I slow down?"

She shook her head. "No. It's just... I've never seen... you are like one of the statues in the British Museum." She lifted a hand and ran it down his sleek torso.

"And you are a Botticelli." His gaze touched her body, and she knew he meant it. She felt no embarrassment with him and no fear. She knew what was coming, and she wanted it. She wanted him.

He stood and removed his trousers, and she made no effort to look away from his erection. It was as beautiful as the rest of him. When he climbed back into the bed, he was warm and solid against her. She wrapped her legs around him and offered her mouth. He took it with his own, kissing her and stroking her body with his hands until she was whimpering with need. Only when she thought she could take no more, did he slide into her, filling her so completely that she gasped at the fierceness of the pleasure rippling through her.

"Not yet," he whispered, moving inside her with slow, tantalizing strokes. He took her hands and clasped them on either side of her head. His eyes locked with hers, and in his gaze she saw desire and pleasure and a need that matched her own.

Finally, his jaw clenched, and he growled low. "Now."

He thrust into her, and she came apart in his arms.

***

Lucien had never been known for moderation. When he enjoyed a pastime, like riding or drinking or fencing, he gave it all of his time and attention. He enjoyed Cassandra in his bed. She was such a mixture of innocence and experience, such an apt pupil and a tender instructor.

He did not want to give her over to sleep, but when her eyes finally closed on a sigh of pleasure, he knew she needed rest. He lay beside her, watching her in the flickering firelight, wondering if this night was all they would ever have.

He had always known he would have to marry one day. He was the heir to the Glennish throne, after all. When he'd turned five and twenty, his father had told him to "stop dallying and choose a bride."

Lucien would have been happy to oblige, but he couldn't seem to find the right woman. He'd courted foreign princesses, duchesses from his own land, and even peasant women. He'd considered women who were friends, including his sisters' closest friends. But no woman had captured his interest. No woman until now.

Cassandra was everything he wanted in a woman, in a wife. Ironic that he should find her when he no longer needed a wife, when the throne was no longer his to claim.

Not only did he not need a queen, he could not justify marrying her when he had nothing to offer her. He had no name, no money, and his meager earnings gained from tutoring would not feed a cat, much less a family. It was wrong to want her, and yet he could not seem to put the feelings aside.

That did not mean he had not protected her from the consequences of their joining. After she'd climaxed, he'd pulled out and spilled his seed on the bed. He did not want to saddle her with a royal bastard, especially one hunted by assassins.

After their lovemaking, he did not sleep, though his body wept with joy at the comfort of the bed. Instead, he held her in his arms, and when it was close to morning, he woke her with a kiss. "Your staff will arise soon. You should return to your chamber."

She kissed him back, her sweet lips so tender against his. "I don't want to leave you."

"Then stay, and we shall shock them all."

She smiled. "How I would love to see the look on Effie's face. But I don't want anything to detain us since we are to go to the bookshop this morning. Effie's lectures can be rather lengthy."

"Then I shall see you again at breakfast."

She kissed him again and was gone.

A footman brought him fresh clothing and clean water to shave and wash, and when they set out in the carriage for Duke Street, he felt almost like himself again.

The snow had finally stopped, but all of London sparkled under a cover of clean white. The horses' bells jingled, reminding him of sleigh rides back home.

At the thought, a pang of sorrow rose in his chest, and at the same time Cassandra put a hand on his arm. She seemed to know when he needed her touch.

"We will find the book" she said, as though she had no doubt in her mind. "Tomorrow is Christmas. I believe we are due a miracle."

He did not believe in miracles, not until he had met her. The coach stopped before On the Shelf, and the coachman opened the carriage door.

"The sign says closed, my lady. That board there is covering the front window."

"Knock anyway, John Coachman. Tell them Lady Ashbrooke must see them."

The coachman shrugged and did as he was told. He banged for several minutes before the door finally opened and a dusty, silver-haired Mr. Merriweather stood in the doorway.

The coachman pointed to the carriage, and Lucien alighted, assisting Cassandra down after.

"Oh, not you again," Merriweather said, frowning at Lucien. "The shop is closed today. We're making repairs, and it's Christmas Eve. A man has a right to spend Christmas Eve with his family."

"I agree with you, Mr. Merriweather," Cassandra said, "but I wonder if you might speak with us for just a few moments. I would be so grateful."

Merriweather was not about to turn away the gratitude of a viscountess. "Of course, my lady. My wife just made tea. Would you like some?"

The three of them sat down to tea in the small office behind the counter. Lucien had had glimpses of the office before, but this was the first time he'd been inside. It was small but tidy, everything in its place. It smelled of tobacco, and indeed Merriweather's pipe rested on the desk. Lucien had rather hoped the office might be wild and unkempt. Then he could believe that an auction slip could be lost. But this was not the sort of room where anything would be lost.

"As you know, Mr. Glen is searching for some rather rare books," Cassandra told Merriweather after they'd sipped tea and talked of the weather. Apparently, it had not snowed in London for years.

"He's in here almost every day. I know that much."

Lucien opened his mouth to say that if the Merriweathers would just tell him where they'd put the books they'd bought at auction, he would gladly leave and not return. He would have been happy never to set foot in another bookshop for the rest of his life.

Cassandra spoke first. "A good friend of his died recently, and the man had borrowed several books belonging to Mr. Glen. All of the man's belongings were auctioned, including the books. Mr. Glen would like the volumes returned. They are not valuable, but they have sentimental meaning to Mr. Glen." She smiled at him. "We will of course pay for the books. And for your trouble, I am willing to give you double what you paid at auction."

"No!" Lucien would not take her money, not that he had his own, but he would work out some sort of trade with the shop owner. In fact, he didn't even need the book, just the papers inside.

"You may pay me back, Mr. Glen," Cassandra said firmly.

"I would, of course, but I would prefer to work out a trade with Mr. Merriweather. I don't want charity."

Merriweather held up a hand, silencing them before the discussion could continue. "I'm afraid you are arguing over nothing, Lady Ashbrooke. I do not have the books you speak of. I rarely buy any books at auction. I much prefer to have the latest novels on hand, rather than invest in any more dusty tomes." He indicated the shop and the shelves of unbound books, their pages between boards until they were purchased and bound by the new owner.

Lucien had probably looked through every single bound and unbound book in the store. If Merriweather did not have any stock in reserve, the books Lucien's mother had sent were not here. He might as well just accept that they were gone forever.

Cassandra's smile faltered. "I see. And there can be no mistake."

"No, my lady." Merriweather straightened officiously. "None."

Lucien rose. No point in sitting here sipping tea. His world had ended. He did not know what he would do now, but he wouldn't spend another minute in the *bluidy* bookshop.

Cassandra rose too, and Merriweather showed them back into the shop and to the door. She and Merriweather were still chatting amiably, but to Lucien they sounded incredibly distant. The crumbling sound of the rest of his life falling to ruins deafened him.

"I'm terribly… window," Cassandra said.

"Catch… culprits," Merriweather answered.

Lucien closed his eyes and attempted to concentrate. He should listen to news of the assassins.

"This isn't the first time the shop has been vandalized, after all."

"Really?" Cassandra asked. "Was it the same window?"

"No. It was the sign. Some fool thought it would be jolly good fun to paint over the name of the shop, owing to the number of more seasoned ladies who patronize us. Turned out we all rather liked the new name and kept On the Shelf."

Lucien stilled, the roaring in his ears subsiding. "What was the name before?"

"What's that?" Merriweather asked.

Lucien clenched his fists to keep from grasping the owner by the lapels and shoving him against the door.

"What. Was. The. Original. Name?"

"Oh, The Duke Street Bookshop. Not very clever, eh? There's another shop with the same name on the Duke Street near the northeast corner of Grosvenor Square."

"Oh my God." Cassandra's gaze met his, and it was only the blue of her eyes that kept his world from spinning. "Yes, of course. There is another Duke Street. It runs from Grosvenor Square, crosses Oxford Street, and ends at Manchester Square. I forgot all about it. I haven't been to the bookshop there in some years."

Lucien's limbs were paralyzed. Another Duke Street. Another bookshop.

"That's the shop that must have bought the auctioned books," Cassandra said.

Merriweather considered. "It's possible. Certainly possible."

Cassandra gripped Merriweather's hand, shaking it vigorously. "Thank you." She turned to Lucien. "Let's go. Now."

"Best hurry," Merriweather advised. "It's Christmas Eve. Most shops will close a bit early."

"Of course." She all but dragged Lucien out of the shop and into the coach. She gave the coachman the direction and turned to Lucien. "This is it. I know we will find the books now."

For the first time in weeks, he had the same hope. Overwhelmed with sudden joy, he pulled her into his arms and kissed her. "Thank you. I owe you everything."

She blushed, whether from the compliment or his kiss, he did not know. "It is I who owe you everything. You've given me so much more than I ever could have expected." Before he could ask what she meant, she pointed out various landmarks to him. They were heading back toward her town house until they turned onto what she said was the other Duke Street. Finally, the coach stopped in front of the shop.

It was larger than On the Shelf and better maintained. Lucien supposed the patrons were wealthier and expected as much. As soon as they entered, Cassandra approached the shopgirl and gave her the same story about Lucien's friend and the auctioned books. Again, she offered to pay double the auction price, which Lucien would have never allowed, but the young woman, who had dark hair in a braid on top of her head, waved a hand in dismissal. "If we have them, you're welcome to them. Never want to take another's property, and it's Christmas Eve, after all."

"Where would they be?" Cassandra asked.

She furrowed a brow and tucked a pencil in the coil on her head. "You said they were books in French and Glennish?"

"That's correct," Lucien said, finding his voice once again.

She smiled at him. "Oh, then you want to look on that last shelf to the left. We keep the foreign books there. We have quite a few Frenchies come in, we do."

"Thank you."

With single-minded purpose, Lucien set off in the direction the shopgirl indicated. His fear now was that the books his mother had sent had been purchased. What if he'd come this far for naught? Finding the books wasn't simply a matter of papers and money any longer. They were the last and only reminders of his mother, his family. He needed to touch those books, touch the papers she'd caressed and so lovingly set aside for her family.

He stood before the shelves and stared at the rows of books. Where to begin? The shop would close soon. He had no time to waste debating. Lucien felt a warm hand clasp his. Cassandra was beside him, smiling up at him. He couldn't help but smile back at her. Her small gesture of support meant more to him than he could possibly express in words.

"I'll start on this side, and you start on that," she suggested.

He nodded his agreement. With trembling hands, he skimmed his fingers over the titles of the old books. Italian titles, German titles, Portuguese...

"Lucien."

His attention snapped to Cassandra, kneeling on the floor, her skirts spread around her.

"I've found the books in Glennish."

He dropped to his knees beside her. He pulled the first book off the shelf, the familiar language like coming home as he read the title. *A Natural History of Glynaven.* He stared at the cover, wondering if this was one of the books his mother had sent. Was this one she had touched?

"Shall I?" Cassandra asked, holding a hand out.

"Please."

She opened it, shuffling through the pages. Before she finished, he knew it was not one of them.

"Oy! We're closing soon!" the shopgirl called.

"Damn it all to hell," Lucien muttered. Why did it seem as though everything, even time, was against him?

"Which one next?" Cassandra asked, her voice as level and calm as ever.

Lucien looked at the other Glennish titles on the shelf. It might be one of them or none of them. His mother might very well have hidden the papers in one of the French books or one in English. Good God, he would never find it if it was one of the English books.

*Think, Lucien! Think.* He'd been standing in her private chamber in the palace when his mother secreted the papers. He could remember the scent of candle wax and roses. He could hear the ripping sound when she'd torn the pages out of the book. If only he'd paid attention to the book, known what it looked like. He was running out of time. He willed the book to be there, scanned the titles, then paused.

*A Collection of Poems for Children.*

"There," he said, reaching for the volume wedged in the corner. A volume with gold lettering and a tattered cover.

"Is that it?" Cassandra asked when he didn't open it right away.

He stared at the book, his hands shaking so badly he feared he'd drop the book. Of course she would have chosen this book. It had been a favorite of the royal children, and his mother had read it to them before bed when they'd been younger.

Lucien met Cassandra's gaze, and her hands slid over his trembling ones. "Open it," she whispered.

How would he have done this without her?

He opened the book. The first page was familiar to him, not only the title but the scribbles his sister Vivi had made one afternoon when she'd found a pen and ink.

He stared at those scribbles, at the evidence of his past life. In the last few months, he'd almost feared he'd dreamed he'd once been a prince, once been the heir to the throne of Glynaven.

He turned several pages, his hands moving more quickly and surely now. He knew who he was, and he knew what he would find in the center of the book. Still, when he reached the space made by the extracted pages, he felt a shock rush through him. He must have jerked, because the papers fell out, Cassandra reaching to catch them before they could land on the floor.

She beamed up at him, her smile so large he had to smile back. "We found them!" she squealed.

He dropped the book and opened the first yellowed paper. It was a letter of introduction for the family, including himself. It had been written in his mother's hand, and he ran a fingertip over his name.

"There is the name of a bank here and an account number. At least I think that is what it is. I cannot read Glennish."

"That is exactly what it is. The Bank of England," he said. He'd known it would be the Old Lady of Threadneedle Street, but his efforts to access the bank accounts of the royal family had been in vain without any papers or the account numbers.

"Oh, and here is a five-pound note. Goodness. If anyone else had found this, he would have thought himself the luckiest man alive."

He took her hand. "I am the luckiest man alive because I have you."

"Me? I didn't do anything."

"You never doubted me," he said, bringing her hand to his lips. "You never once doubted me. That faith means more to me than gold."

"Shall we go to the bank?" she asked, her gaze lowering as though she was embarrassed. "We should hurry if we want to arrive before they close for the holiday."

He'd forgotten time was not on his side. He'd forgotten the assassins were still searching for him. The sooner he went to the bank and distanced himself from Cassandra, the safer she would be. Every minute spent with her put her in danger.

At one time this foray to the bank would have been all that mattered to him. He would have run all the way there. Now he did not want to rise, did not want to begin the trip.

He knew every minute closer to the bank was one last minute spent with Cassandra.

## Chapter Seven

They'd raced to the bank for naught. If Cassandra could have beaten the bank manager with a birch, she would have done so. Now that they were back in the carriage and returning to her town house—the book, papers, and money clutched in Lucien's hands—she could admit he had reined in his temper far better than she.

"I do apologize for my outburst," she said. "I'm certain Mr. Sutton has no idea what came over me. I have known him for years and never so much as raised my voice."

His mouth twitched as though he wanted to smile but would not allow himself to do so. "You have nothing to apologize for," he said again. "In fact, you were quite magnificent."

She was about to deny it, when he crossed the carriage and pulled her into his arms. She loved being in his arms. They were strong and so very warm. When she was in his embrace, nothing else mattered. Not Effie's disapproval when they returned home, not the ridiculous bank manager who would not see them on Christmas Eve, not the fact that Lucien was leaving her.

He hadn't said as much, but she knew it. He'd said good-bye with his eyes a thousand times. He worried for her safety. He worried he asked too much of her. He was not good at accepting charity from others. He did not want to impose on her.

If he'd have but listened, she would have told him it was no imposition. She would have told him she never wanted him to leave. Unfortunately, his sense of honor would force him to keep her safe from the assassins targeting him. It was honor that would force him to leave. He didn't love her, else he would not have been able to go away.

She loved him. Completely. And she was a weak, desperate woman. So desperate, in fact, that she did the one thing she'd been telling herself she must not do.

"Stay with me tonight."

He drew back. "Cassandra, it's not safe for me to be near you."

"I don't care about safe. Lucien, it's Christmas Eve. You cannot spend it alone."

But of course he could. He had money now. He would find a room in a hotel and sleep in comfort. The unspoken words were hers.

*Don't leave me alone.*

Another solitary Christmas, listening to the servants' games and wishing she had someone to kiss under the mistletoe.

She turned to look out the windows at the dusky evening quickly falling. The last rays of sunlight made the melting snow sparkle.

"Cassandra." His tone was placating, asking for understanding.

For once she would not accommodate. She would not be placated. She would ask for what she wanted, and she would have it too. "Stay with me," she said, looking at him again. "Come to my bed. Make love to me this one last night. Surely even assassins do not work on Christmas."

He gave a small bark of laughter, then gathered her into his embrace. "How will I ever leave you? Yes, fair Cassandra, I'll stay with you tonight."

The simple words made the rest of the long evening bearable—Effie's hysterics, the awkward Christmas Eve dinner afterward, the stilted singing of carols when the Yule log was brought inside. Cass had been relieved to retire as early as Effie and leave the servants to their revelry. Lucien had retired before either of them, and she lay in her large bed for an hour before he finally tapped on her door and slid inside. Cass had gone to him the night before for fear Effie would know she was with the prince, but Cass no longer cared about Effie's opinion. Effie's behavior then had been nothing short of embarrassing. Cass no longer felt she owed her late husband's sister anything but the most common courtesy.

She sat. "I thought perhaps you'd fallen asleep."

He wore no coat, and he drew his shirt over his head as he approached the bed. "The thought of you kept me wide awake."

Cassandra swallowed at the sight of him as he stalked across the room, his broad shoulders tapering into a lean waist and slim hips encased in tight breeches. Lord but she did love to look at him. He had to be leaner than before he'd fled Glynaven. He must be nothing short of a god when in top form.

He watched her watch him as he raised a hand to the fall of the breeches. "It took me a moment to find your room. I fear I almost disturbed Miss Ashbrooke's peace."

Cass giggled at the idea. Effie would have perished from merely the thought of a man touching her.

The bed sagged under Lucien's weight as he sat to remove his boots. They were his own and quite tightly fitted. He had to struggle for a moment before he finally shed them. Then he stood again, but Cass caught his hand before he reached for his breeches.

He raised a brow. "Too presumptuous of me?"

How could the man possibly think she—any woman, really—would not want him in her bed? "Not at all. I want to do it myself."

She bit her lip to stem the rising flush. She had promised herself she would ask for what she wanted, and damn the mortification. He'd looked so beautiful last night, rising proudly from the juncture of his muscled thighs.

"I am at your disposal, my lady," he said, all graciousness.

She sat up, and the sheets fell down about her waist. Lucien drew in a sharp breath at her nudity. "I see I was not being presumptuous at all."

"I thought this might save us time."

"In a hurry, are we?"

"Just eager."

He made a low sound of agreement in his throat. "Then touch me."

She'd seen his hands shake at the bookshop this morning, and now her hands shook as she took hold of the fall of his breeches. She felt like a virgin as she unfastened them and slid the clothing down over his hips, freeing his hard member.

He was aroused, by her. He wanted her. She could see it in the way he clenched his hands to give her time to touch him, the way his eyes devoured her body, the way he groaned when she stroked his manhood.

"You will be my undoing," he said finally, after she'd explored every hard inch of him, cupping the soft underside and even running her tongue along the shiny tip. "I want to touch you. Let me make you ready, and then I promise I'll allow you to have your way with me."

His words, though partly in jest, sent a shiver of excitement through her. His gaze slid to her suddenly hard nipples. "Oh, you like that idea, I see. Far be it from me to deny you anything at Christmas."

He touched her then, his large hands cupping her face so he could kiss her as deeply and thoroughly as he wanted. And then those hands were on her breasts, giving them the aching relief they needed but stroking a stronger need in her too. Finally, after forays to her belly, her legs, her buttocks, he cupped her between her legs, touching her in the place that throbbed for him.

"Yes," she moaned, letting her head fall back and shamelessly rocking her body against his skilled fingers. He'd been kneeling before her, but now he skated his hands up and took her by the waist. He pulled her onto his lap, situating her so his erection brushed the tingling spot where his fingers had been.

"Put your arms around me," he ordered. She wrapped her arms about his shoulders, clasping her hands behind his head and feeling the tips of her breasts brush against his solid chest.

He kissed her, shifting her so her legs parted farther.

"Take me inside you," he murmured, nipping at her jaw. "Give yourself the pleasure your body is yearning for."

She was yearning. Everything in her reached and groped for that elusive pleasure. All she need do was rise up and tilt forward. His tip slid inside her, and she gasped at the beauty of it, of the feel of him inside her. She lowered herself, feeling him stretch her, fill her, claim her.

Her body moved without her telling it to. Her hips circled and thrust, and every single groan he made gratified her. His hands on her back tightened until the pressure of his fingers was all that anchored her.

"Lucien," she gasped when she could not contain the spiraling feelings building in her any longer.

"You are beautiful, Cassandra. So beautiful."

Her body unraveled then. Strand by delicate strand, tendrils of pleasure flowed through her until she practically sobbed with the exquisite torture of it.

Afterward, she was so boneless she slumped against him, and he rolled her onto her side, his arms coming around her to press her to his chest. She buried her face in the scent of him—the scent of both of them mingled together.

"I love you," she whispered. She shouldn't have said it, but she couldn't let him go without saying it.

"Yes," he said, and stroked her hair. "Yes."

***

He was not a rake, but he knew very well how to play the part. Christmas morning he played it well. He rose long before Cassandra, trying very hard not to admire the way the first glimmerings of pale morning light washed the soft slopes of her back and hips.

He dressed in silence and crept out of her room, not to his own chamber, but downstairs, where the only servant about—a weary maid—glanced at him quickly before looking back at the fireplace she was lighting.

He put a finger to his lips and crossed to the front door. He unlocked it silently and paused before pulling it open. He should have left a note. Bloody hell, the woman had told him she loved him.

He loved her too—God, how he loved her—but he could not afford to love anyone or anything at the moment. If he loved her, he would leave her. Yes, it would mean giving up the hope of finding the articles he could only access with the papers his mother had left him, but those mattered nothing when he thought of the danger to Cassandra. Perhaps one day he could come back to her. One day, when assassins were no longer a threat, he could knock on her door again. She might welcome him back. She might still love him.

If she ever forgave him this treachery.

He opened the door and stood in it, dumbfounded. A coach with a ducal crest sat in front of the town house. Lucien watched the footman jump down and make for the door, indicating the conveyance had only just arrived. The door opened before the footman could reach it, and a well-dressed, fair-haired man stepped out. He waved the footman away and held out a hand. A gloved hand gripped it from inside the curtained coach, and then a woman with a hat that covered her face emerged. Cassandra had not said anything about guests, most especially not a duke. He wavered, torn between going back and leaving as planned.

And then the woman looked up, and his world flipped upside down.

She seemed equally shocked, staring at him in silence, almost as though she had seen a ghost. He knew the feeling. He'd thought she was dead. He'd already mourned her, and now to see her standing there, very much alive, was both confusing and an extraordinary relief.

"Lucien!"

He didn't so much hear the word as he saw her mouth move. The man looked at him with interest, and Lucien had a moment to wonder who the devil he was and why he thought he had the right to touch her.

And then she was rushing toward him, and he didn't think anymore. He met her in the middle of the walk, racing to embrace her and twirl her in his arms.

She laughed and kissed both of his cheeks, repeatedly. On a laugh, she said, "I thought you were dead."

"I thought *you* were dead." His eyes stung with what felt suspiciously like tears. He had honestly never thought he would see her again, would never see anyone from his past life again.

"I cannot believe it is you. Let me look at you." She cupped his face and looked long and hard into his eyes. When she had seen whatever she searched for, she hugged him again. Hard. "My poor darling. What you have suffered. I can only imagine."

Behind her, the man, presumably the duke, approached. As though she sensed his presence, she turned. "Nathan, I have forgotten my manners completely."

"It's quite understandable."

Nathan? Lucien narrowed his eyes. Exactly who was this man?

"Prince Lucien Charles Louis de Glynaven, this is my husband, Nathan Cauley, Duke of Wyndover."

"Your husband?" Lucien stared hard at the man.

The duke bowed. "It's a pleasure to make your acquaintance. Your sister did not sleep at all last night, I'm afraid. We received a letter from the manager of the Bank of England that you were alive. He thought you were an impostor."

"I know this is terribly early, but I couldn't wait another moment." She glanced at the house behind him. "Mr. Sutton mentioned you were with Lady Ashbrooke, but how is it you have come to reside in her home?"

"How is it you are married?"

She laughed again, a sound so familiar to him, he wanted to hug her again. Vivi was alive.

"I see we have much to discuss. Might we go inside, where it is warmer? Or must you be away?"

"I..." What to say? That he was sneaking away like some sort of thief? "There are assassins in London," he said finally.

The duke lifted a finger, and his outriders jumped down. "Watch the house," he commanded. "Keep the horses moving. I don't want the carriage spotted outside."

The four outriders spread out along the front of the house, while the coachman urged the horses to walk.

Well, they were safe enough, but Lucien could hardly invite guests into Cassandra's home. "Very good," he said. "Now there is just the matter of Lady Ashbrooke."

"And what matter might that be?" said a voice from behind.

It was her, of course. She'd probably heard the horses and the voices. The entire house probably had. He turned. "Happy Christmas."

"Is it?" Her blue eyes were wary. She'd dressed in haste, her lavender gown wrinkled and her feet bare. Her hair fell in golden waves down about her shoulders.

"It is," Vivi said, flashing the smile she always gave when she wanted to charm someone. "This morning I have the best Christmas present I could ever hope for. My brother is alive."

She looked at Lucien, who gave her a nod. "Princess Vivienne Aubine Calanthe de Glynaven, this is Lady Ashbrooke. Lady Ashbrooke, my sister and her husband, His Grace, the Duke of Wyndover."

He wasn't certain if he'd done all the introductions correctly. He couldn't remember the exact protocol the English used.

Cassandra curtseyed. "Please, come in out of the cold and wet." She indicated the few piles of slush that were all that remained of the recent snows.

Lucien had expected Cassandra to be less than hospitable. After all, she'd awakened Christmas morning to find her lover had fled and unexpected guests at her door. Not to mention, she was short-staffed since she had given some of the staff the day off. It was also no secret that her late husband's sister was silently protesting Lucien's arrival by keeping to her room.

But she made the best of it, going to the kitchens herself to ask for tea and scones and listening attentively to Vivi's story. She'd been in the palace during the massacre and had escaped by hiding in the secret room. He did not ask her for the details of what she had seen and heard. He would ask her later, when they were both stronger and ready to confront that horrible time again. Their father's trusted adviser, Masson, had helped her to safety in England before assassins had killed him. She and Wyndover had confronted three other assassins at his estate in Nottinghamshire. That explained why Wyndover traveled with additional guards.

After Lucien had also told his story, Cassandra, who had been quietly attentive, cleared her throat. "Princess, do you mind if I ask how you knew to find Lu—your brother here?"

Vivi withdrew the letter the bank manager had sent, whereupon Lucien showed his sister and the duke the papers he and Cassandra had found at the bookshop.

"But this is remarkable!" Vivi said. "We must see what is in that account."

"Unfortunately, the bank is not open today. It's Christmas," Cassandra pointed out.

Vivi looked at the duke. He gave a sigh. "Give me a moment. May I borrow pen and paper?" he asked.

Cassandra directed him to the small desk in the corner of the parlor where they sat. Vivi followed him, watching over his shoulder as, presumably, he summoned the bank manager to the bank with the sorts of promises and threats only a duke can make.

"Would you ever have told me good-bye?" Cassandra hissed at Lucien when the duke was fully engaged in his task.

Lucien passed a hand over his eyes. "I should have left a note."

"Saying what?" she asked under her breath. "Thank you and Happy Christmas?"

"No." He rose from the chair where he was seated and joined her on the couch. "I would have said, I am sorry to have endangered your life. I was weak and foolish. I'll leave now before I do you any further harm."

She stared at him. "You are an idiot."

Lucien blew out a breath. He had expected gratitude or, at the very least, understanding. "For trying to keep you safe?"

"No. For not understanding that you mean more to me than my own safety. That I understood the cost long before now and made the choice to help you anyway. I told you I love you, Lucien. Doesn't that mean anything?"

"Yes." It did. It meant everything. He loved her too. That was why he had to leave her. "That is exactly why I had to go," he began.

She looked stricken, but before he could explain further, Wyndover stood. "I'll send this directly. The bank manager will meet us with all haste, I assure you."

Lucien wished he could have seen the missive, but the duke carried it to the door, where presumably he handed it to one of his men to deliver.

Vivi lifted her reticule. "Shall we go? I think it's past time we saw what Mama has sent us from the grave."

# Chapter Eight

If Cass had not wanted to hit Lucien, hard, she would have enjoyed the duke's carriage. It was delightfully luxurious with velvet squabs, brocade draperies, lovely brass lamps, and a silk interior. The footman gave them all warm bricks wrapped in cloth and cozy blankets. Cass thought the conveyance warmer and better appointed than her town house.

The men sat across from her and the princess, which made hitting Lucien more difficult. Unfortunately, it also made it easier to see his face. His beautiful eyes were filled with regret and apology. Apology for what? For leaving her or not loving her? She had said she loved him, and the words had driven him away. He was an honorable man. She had always known that. If he couldn't love her, he would rather leave her than stay and give her false hope.

Perhaps she should have stayed home and allowed him to leave with his sister. That would have saved both of them the awkwardness of a good-bye. But she hadn't been able to do it. She was a foolish, weak woman. She did not want to let him go yet. When he left, her life would return to the way it had been.

No, she would not go back to wearing widow's weeds. In fact, it had felt wonderful to dress in this lavender gown, though it was desperately in need of pressing. No, she wouldn't go back to bowing and cringing when Effie spoke, or trying to make herself invisible so she would not trouble anyone else.

But she would go back to a life devoid of passion. Her clothing might not be drab, but her life would lose all its color when Lucien was gone. She would rather be dead than suffer that fate.

She heard a loud explosion, and one of the horses screamed and reared. Vivienne cried out, and then everything was a blur of velvet and gold as the carriage tilted to the side before righting itself again. Cass pressed her hands to her ears to drown out the screeching sound before she realized it was she making the awful noise.

She clamped a hand over her mouth, holding in her screams. Her chest hurt from the way her heart slammed against it. Wyndover scrambled to draw his pistol as Lucien parted the curtains. Cass wanted to order him to close the curtains, to hide, but she couldn't seem to utter any sounds other than screams. Beside her, the princess reached under the seat and withdrew a bow and arrows.

Cass half expected to wake at any moment, but when she heard another explosion and a man's anguished cry, she knew this was no dream.

"*Le reavlutionnaire!*" Lucien shouted right before he pulled her and the princess to the ground. The window of the coach shattered, and Cass couldn't hold back her cry.

More deafening sounds erupted. Cass looked up to see the duke lowering his pistol from the broken window. "Missed. Damn it!"

"Stay down," Lucien ordered her.

Another pistol ball slammed into the coach, and Wyndover knelt beside her, adding powder and shot to his pistol. Meanwhile, the princess had withdrawn an arrow and nocked it against her bowstring.

"Careful, love," Wyndover cautioned.

"Always." Then she was up, and quick as a cat, she fired the arrow and ducked down again. Another explosion, this one rocking the coach again, and then Wyndover was up, firing through the window.

The duke flattened himself, but there was no return fire.

"I think I hit one." The princess sounded hopeful.

"*You* hit?" Her husband scowled at her. "Perhaps it was my pistol ball."

"Darling, you know I never miss."

Cass tentatively raised her head. Lucien's body shielded her from harm, but he rose slightly to allow her to look up.

"Stay down," he told her again. "They might be waiting for us to step out."

"Good point." Wyndover withdrew his powder bag again. "One of us will have to go out and assess the damage. I fear my coachman is dead."

"I'll go," his wife offered.

Lucien uttered a word Cass did not know. "No, you will not. I'll go."

The princess looked at him as though he'd grown horns. "You don't even have a weapon."

"I—"

The door upon which Cass's shoulder rested flew open, and she nearly spilled out into an assassin's arms. Wyndover and the princess, who had been expecting another attack from the opposite side where the first shots had been fired, were unprepared. Cass screamed, right before she was yanked out by her hair. She would have fallen to the ground, but Lucien caught her arm.

For a moment, a dreadful and painful tug-of-war ensued, and then one of the princess's arrows whizzed by, hitting the man holding her in the shoulder. He dropped her, and Lucien lost his hold. Cass tumbled to the ground. Her shoulder gave a violent scream of pain, but she managed to ignore it long enough to look about. Two more assassins headed for her. The first, a very large man, looked more angry than injured by the arrow in his shoulder. He ripped it out and growled at her.

With a swipe, he reached for her hair again, but Cass rolled away and under the carriage. She saw a blur of movement, and the assassin landed on his back beside the carriage, Lucien on top of him.

More shots rang out, and Cass was not certain if they came from Wyndover or the remaining assassins. Her gaze was riveted on Lucien, who fought the huge assassin valiantly but was losing ground. The assassin gave a heave, and Lucien flew off him, flipping onto his back. He lay stunned for a moment.

Behind him, another assassin came around the front of the carriage, his pistol in his hands.

"Lucien! Behind you!" Cass yelled.

Lucien rolled just in time, and the pistol ball hit the ground where he had been a moment before. He grabbed the man's ankles and brought him down, but now the other, injured assassin had gained his feet. He lumbered toward Lucien, hauled him up by the neck, and lifted him off the ground.

"No!" Cass screamed. "He's choking him!"

Another arrow whizzed from the coach, but it hit the third assassin, preventing him from joining his comrades attacking the prince.

"Shoot him!" the princess cried.

"I can't get a shot! Bloody hell!"

Lucien's body looked like that of a rag doll in the large assassin's bloody hands. Lucien clawed and fought, his movements erratic. Any shot the duke fired at the assassin might also hit Lucien.

Lucien didn't have time to wait until the assassin moved into the line of fire. Cass was not about to allow him to die on Christmas Day, there in the middle of London. She had no weapon, but that didn't seem to matter. She crawled out from under the coach and rushed toward the assassin holding Lucien. With a shriek, she jumped onto his back.

"Lady Ashbrooke! No!" the duchess called.

It was too late. She couldn't turn back now.

The assassin tried to shake her off. She slid down his back, but before she could fall off, she wrapped her arms around his neck and squeezed. He staggered, releasing Lucien.

The other assassin promptly swung at the prince, and Cass only knew the blow landed because she heard the thud. The assassin shook her violently, but she locked her hands and closed her eyes. Wetness dribbled over her wrists, and she realized it was the blood from the arrow wound.

More thuds. Another pistol shot. A man—or was it a woman?—yelped. Cass screeched too, squeezing with everything she had. The assassin stumbled to his knees. She felt the arrow whoosh past her and heard the thunk as it made contact.

And then Lucien was calling her name. "Cassandra! Let go. I have him. Let go. Cassandra!"

She let go, sliding to the ground.

Lucien raised a boot and kicked the assassin, and he fell beside her. His eyes met hers briefly before they rolled back and closed.

For a long moment, all she heard was her own panting breaths. And then she was in Lucien's arms, her face pressed against his chest. She heard the solid beat of his heart, and nothing else mattered.

\*\*\*

"*Leannan*. My love." Lucien cradled Cassandra. "What the devil were you thinking?"

He'd almost lost her. Twice. He knew his sister was absolutely—what was the English word? Daft?—but she was skilled with a bow and arrow and could defend herself. Cassandra had no such skills, which made her efforts to save him that much more meaningful.

She'd risked her life for him.

And he had been ready to leave her because he had no kingdom. What did such things matter? He'd wanted to keep her safe, but the assassins had found them anyway. Together they'd defeated the enemy.

He looked up from where his cheek was pressed against her hair, assessing the bodies strewn around them. Five men lay dead or wounded. Vivienne had an arrow pointed at one, and her duke trained a pistol on another. The two beside him were not moving, and the last looked dead or dying from his wounds.

"He was choking you," Cassandra said. "I had to do something."

Lucien realized she was answering his question.

"You risked your life." That was more than obvious, but he still couldn't quite believe it.

"So did you," she said, her tone full of accusation. She looked up at him. At some point, her spectacles had fallen off, and her blue eyes looked so naked and vulnerable without them. "I couldn't let him kill you. I told you. I love you."

"*Leannan.* Don't you know by now that I love you too? I couldn't live with myself if anything happened to you. I was afraid of this"—he waved a hand—"I was afraid I'd lose you."

"The risk is worth the gain," she said.

"You are a wise woman, Lady Ashbrooke, and you were right."

"About?"

"I am an idiot."

She laughed, a tear falling on one pink cheek. "Yes, you are."

"Will you have me anyway?"

She blinked, looking at him long and hard. "Do you mean..."

"Will you be my princess? You'd be a princess of a lost kingdom, but that's all I have to offer."

"If I have you, Lucien, that's all I need."

\*\*\*

Nothing could ruin Christmas night for Cass. Not Effie's declaration that her brother's will stipulated she was to have the town house if Cass remarried. Not the throbbing pain in her arms from gripping that assassin so tightly. Not the hours of questioning they'd endured from Bow Street, who had taken the assassins into custody.

Lucien had his papers and the contents of the vault his mother had entrusted to the bank. The bank manager had tried to protest, tried to insinuate Lucien was an impostor, but the duke had said something to the man in low tones, and he hadn't uttered another word after that.

Now she and Lucien sat in her bedroom with the contents of the vault laid on the bed before them. A large purse held thousands in pounds, and there were other accounts as well. Lucien had access to all of them and was a very rich man. Perhaps not as rich as he would have been if he'd been king of Glynaven, but rich nonetheless.

Several miniatures had also been included, paintings of all his brothers and sisters and his mother and father. Lucien had looked at them for a long time before putting them down. "I will share these with Vivienne," he'd said solemnly.

Other treasures abounded, including jewels and priceless heirlooms. Lucien had barely glanced at them, but Cassandra was a bit awestruck at the amount of glitter on her coverlet.

"This is the last of it," Lucien said, indicating a small wooden box with an intricately carved pattern of ivy on the sides and top.

"What do you think is inside?"

"I have no idea."

He opened it, unclasping the latch quietly and raising the lid. He stared down at it for a moment, then smiled.

Cass did not have the patience to wait. "Well?"

"Bits of lace from her coronation dress and her favorite jeweled combs. I will give those to Vivienne. And then there is this smaller box. This is for you."

He held it up, a small box covered in green satin with gold braid.

"For me? I didn't know your mother."

"But she knew one day I would find you." He removed the top of the box, and inside shone a ring with a large oval emerald set in gold, the gem surrounded by glittering diamonds.

"Oh." That was all she could think to say.

"Come here," Lucien said quietly.

She was already right beside him, but she moved close enough to where he sat on the bed so her knees brushed his.

He lifted her hand and slid the ring on her finger. He stared at it for a long time, then looked up at her. "It fits perfectly."

She tilted the ring so it caught the light. It was impossibly beautiful. "I can't take this. You should give it to Vivienne."

Lucien made a shushing sound. "She will say it should go to my wife. You are my bride-to-be, are you not?"

She nodded. "Yes."

"Then it goes to you, Princess Cassandra. Happy Christmas."

"Happy Christmas. The very happiest." She lifted her aching arms and wrapped them around him, kissing him with peace and joy and, most of all, love.

# Acknowledgments

Thank you to Abby Saul and Joanna MacKenzie for their work
compiling this duet. And I owe much appreciation to Kim Killion
for all her work on this cover and the many others she's done for
me.

Thank you to Susan Knight and the Shananigans for their
help with the title of *A Prince in Her Stocking*. Thank you to my
wonderful readers for their suggestion of *Waiting for a Duke Like
You* as a title.

And thanks to Grace Burrowes, Carolyn Jewel, and Miranda
Neville for all your suggestions and inspiration on both these
novellas.

# About Shana Galen

Shana Galen is the bestselling author of passionate Regency romps, including the RT Reviewers' Choice *The Making of a Gentleman*. Kirkus says of her books, "The road to happily-ever-after is intense, conflicted, suspenseful and fun," and *RT Book Reviews* calls her books "lighthearted yet poignant, humorous yet touching." She taught English at the middle and high school level off and on for eleven years. Most of those years were spent working in Houston's inner city. Now she writes full time. She's happily married and has a daughter who is most definitely a romance heroine in the making.

Wonder what Shana has coming next? Join Shana's <u>mailing list</u>, and be the first to receive information on sales and new releases. Shana never spams or sells readers' information.

# Books by Shana Galen

In the mood for more Christmas love? Check out *All I Want for Christmas is Blue* and *The Spy Beneath the Mistletoe*!

Dive into one of Shana's many series...
> *The Covent Garden Cubs* series begins with *Earls Just Want to Have Fun*.
> *The Lord and Lady Spy* series begins with *Lord and Lady Spy*.
> *The Jewels of the Ton* series begins with *When You Give a Duke a Diamond*.
> *The Sons of the Revolution* series begins with *The Making of a Duchess*.
> *The Misadventures in Matrimony* series begins with *No Man's Bride*.
> *The Regency Spies* series begins with *While You Were Spying*.

Made in the USA
San Bernardino, CA
24 January 2019